About the Author

Dr Daniel Osigbe was born in Lagos, Nigeria, and moved to London at eleven years of age. He went on to study medicine at Kings College London. As well as working as a GP in London, he engages in medical missions and numerous other charity projects.

A Great Man Has Come Home

To Claire

wishing you a fantastic
read

Daniel Osigbe

Dr Daniel Osigbe

A Great Man Has Come Home

Olympia Publishers
London

www.olympiapublishers.com
OLYMPIA PAPERBACK EDITION

A CIP catalogue record for this title is
available from the British Library.

ISBN: 978-1-78830-620-1

This is a work of fiction.
Names, characters, places and incidents originate from the writer's
imagination. Any resemblance to actual persons, living or dead, is
purely coincidental.

First Published in 2020

Olympia Publishers
Tallis House
2 Tallis Street
London
EC4Y 0AB

Printed in Great Britain

Dedication

I dedicate this book to the memory of my father 'Late Chief Lagos Otutu Osigbe', from whose life I draw the inspiration for this book. The principal character is also named after him. I also dedicate this book to my beautiful daughter, Gabi, our joy.

Acknowledgements

I firstly acknowledge God Almighty, with whom nothing is impossible.

Also my dearest wife, who believes in me and allowed me the space to write, despite the birth of our daughter. I would like to also thank my mother, Dorothy, for her love and taking time out to read the early manuscript. Also those that have given me feedback and taken time to read the manuscript, my brother Peter, Abraham, Eji and anyone else I might have forgotten to mention.

Chapter One

Thirty months ago

He sauntered up to the house in Agility, in the Mile Twelve area. He had sat in his car for the last five minutes, admiring the house. A duplex sitting on a piece of land that measured about an acre. Excitingly the duplex occupied sixty percent of the property. Visible from where he sat in his blue Toyota Auris, he could see the upper veranda; it looked like a good sitting place.

He had all the windows wound down; it was a hot day, too hot for the air conditioning when the car wasn't even moving; he could feel the beads of sweat running down the sides of his temple and back of his neck. It was also a good day; the sun was high and there was colour all around: from the palm fronds, to the green shrubbery on the sides of the road, to the white sand that lined the main road.

He liked the property; he had seen the advert in the Vanguard newspaper, which his driver had picked up for him one Friday morning about four months ago now. He had considered a few other properties too. He owned a house where he stayed with his wife and three children.

He wanted to purchase a place for his mistress and her

expected child. A reward for her conception. His second wife whom he married seven years ago had borne no children, definitely no boys.

He had only known her for the last six months; she wasn't his first extra-marital affair. She was different from the others, which was why she was still in the picture. He had been married for about thirteen years now; his first wife had borne three children. His eldest his eleven-year-old daughter, a seven-year-old daughter and the last born a three-year-old girl.

He loved his first wife, that's why they were still married, otherwise he would have married yet another woman. His second wife hadn't borne him a boy; he could not afford to spend so much on bride price to marry someone who wouldn't give him a son. So, this time, a mistress would have to give him a son first. Aside from the lack of a son from his wife, things had now gotten stale; well they went stale about six years ago when he had his first affair. Being with someone younger and half his first wife's age was exhilarating. His current mistress was only twenty-four years old. She was three months pregnant, and hopefully it would be a boy: the boy who would bear his name and inherit the major share of his properties.

He didn't dare to try to have another child with his first wife again. He thought to himself that he couldn't bear the idea of what his friends would say. Two wives and four girls in the house; that would be the death of him. He wouldn't be able to hold his head up at family gatherings; his aged parents would look at him with disdain, wondering if he was carrying some form of a curse.

He had settled on this property before him because it was a good-sized property and it was priced relatively cheaply for what it was. He hadn't almost believed it. A property this size with it divided up into four sections.

The house comprised sixteen bedrooms, six toilets, six bathrooms and three kitchens. Sitting in his car, he could imagine what kind of person lived there. The house was fully plastered but not painted, and some of the windows were old and appeared like they definitely had not been updated in the last twenty years. There was a large red gate to allow cars into the compound and a smaller gate for people to walk through on the left-hand side of the main gate.

Mr Yakubu's car was parked at a strategic spot right at the top of the street. Because it was a straight wide street, he could easily see most of the way up the entire street, especially given his interest was on the opposite side of the road from where he was parked.

It was amazing what he could tell about people from how they dressed, what mannerisms they had, the car they owned, even the house they lived in. He was very good at figuring people out; this was how he got himself where he was today. He vividly remembered when he plotted against the leader of the syndicate he was in. 'Cash boss' they called him. They had worked from Surulere, and their job was simply to convince people in London and the United States to send money to them. Most people would shake their head and think to themselves that only a *mumu* (fool) would fall for such a trick, and most people were right. There were many *mumus* around the world. He had gotten lawyers, doctors and many more to send money to his organisation.

Cash boss was very greedy; he used to pocket sixty percent of the earnings of the syndicate even though there were four members of the syndicate. As well as cash boss, there was their computer whizz Jide, the script writer Ikenna and then himself. He saw himself as the mastermind. After six months of working together he had gotten tired of what he perceived as oppression. He colluded with the other members, and he gave an anonymous tip to MoneyGram about the current account that they used to receive the illicit funds to.

MoneyGram had in turn put a blockade on the particular account and marked it as fraudulent. Then Mr Yakubu gave another anonymous tip to the anti-corruption unit of the Nigerian police, who arrested cash boss as he attended at the bank to collect a sum of two million naira. This led to the arrest and conviction of cash boss. He never found out who tipped the police off as he was thrown into his jail cell. The three remaining members of the syndicate simply opened another account and split the earnings equally three ways.

Things had changed recently; Mr Yakubu had recently disbanded the syndicate. He was planning on running for the seat of councillor in his local government area (LGA) next year, when elections were due. He had to tie up loose ends, there couldn't be any obvious ties to the criminal underworld.

The owner must have been quite wealthy earlier in his life and must have fallen on hard times more recently. This was Nigeria, some things are not always so sure. But Yakubu felt sure of this; it was indeed this mild state of disrepair and lack of grandeur that made the owner put this on the market for just fifty million naira. If he played his cards right, he might be able to negotiate this down to forty million, maybe even thirty-five million naira. It depended on how hard times were for the owner. Equivalent properties he had seen which were painted, and even not as big were on the market for upwards of ninety million naira.

With a bit of paintwork and changing a few features, which should cost him less than a million naira, he could transform this to a grand mansion. A place he could come and live with his mistress, whenever he chose to. Yakubu's second wife hadn't borne any children so the rivalry in his home wasn't that great; he didn't want the *wahala* (stress) of all these women, so he would give this new one her home.

'Driver, drive up to that red gate over there,' Yakubu ordered.

'OK, Sir', his driver responded. The engine kicked back in to life, the driver shifted into drive mode and gently stepped on the accelerator. With a little rumble, the Toyota Auris rumbled gently to the front of the gate. Beep beep, the driver pressed on the horn gently. A couple of minutes later, a tall lean man came down, walked through the side door and walked to the passenger side of the car.

'Good morning, Sah, can I help you? Who are you looking for?'

'I've come to see Mr Otutu,' Yakubu replied. As he spoke, a huge man walked into the upstairs veranda that Yakubu had been admiring, and leaned on its banister, and peered into the road in front of his gate.

Ben looked up and shouted up to the man, 'Daddy, this man has come to see you. Mr Yakubu, he says.'

'OK,' the voice from the veranda boomed. That's what it felt like to Mr Yakubu, and that was the only way to describe it. 'I've been expecting him,' the big man in the veranda boomed again. Mr Yakubu was impressed; there was power in that voice. He could imagine his voice could be heard at the end of the street where he had parked up initially. 'Come up,' the boom came down again after the driver had parked the car.

It was easy to describe it as parking, but there was so much space that the driver simply pressed the footbrake and put the handbrake up when he felt he had entered the compound sufficiently.

Mr Yakubu always wore an expression that suggested he was in charge, but on this day, he felt like there was a mountain before him.

When the driver came out of the vehicle, he made himself comfortable on a stool by the fence where the shadow of the house provided some shade for him. Mr Yakubu followed Ben into the house. There was a front veranda on the ground floor too, which was hemmed in with a metal fence that had started to rust. The gate was for security, otherwise it would have looked so much lovelier without the gate.

Ben led him through a long corridor that ended at a wall, and to his left at the end of the wall was a flight of stairs. On arriving on the top floor, they made the reverse journey down another long corridor to the front upper veranda. On either side of the corridors were doors, which Mr Yakubu believed led to rooms.

When Mr Yakubu arrived upstairs, Mr Otutu stood up from his seat, and boomed, 'Good afternoon, sir, have a sit here please,' while ushering him to the seat farthest away from the doorway. Mr Otutu was wearing a clean white singlet and black pants, and on his feet, he had on black slippers. Mr Yakubu assumed the singlet was due to the temperature. It felt cool up in the veranda.

'I have some refreshment here, so be free,' Pa Otutu said, pointing to an assortment of soft drinks on the table. There were also two small tumblers and a bottle of gin on the small table between them in the veranda.

Though Mr Otutu was quite close to Mr Yakubu and he appeared as though he was speaking normally, his voice still boomed. It hadn't hurt Mr Yakubu's ears, but shook his heart in the same way a gust of wind could cause someone to sway. Mr Otutu was tall and wide, and even his stance had an energetic boom that matched the boom of his voice; there was raw power locked in that body, even at his age.

'You must be Mr Yakubu,' Mr Otutu said. 'Well, welcome. As you can see, we've got some drinks for you and ...' His voice trailed off. After looking at Mr Yakubu for a few seconds, he replaced the lid over the small plate of kola. He always welcomed family with kola; he also welcomed dignitaries and wealthy people with kola because it made them feel he was taking them seriously. However, after looking in Mr Yakubu's eyes he changed his mind. Not that he thought Mr Yakubu didn't have money. He wasn't sure he wanted to welcome him.

For the Urhobos, kola is an important aspect of culture. If an Urhobo person received a personal visit from someone they hadn't seen for a while, the person would not have been welcome if no kola had been presented. For business and strangers, it wasn't essential; however, the Urhobos usually presented kolas to dignitaries and important visitors in order to gain their favour.

So, after drinking, Mr Yakubu began, 'Thanks for welcoming me in such a delightful manner. As you are aware, I have come about your house. I really like it and would like to buy it.'

'Very good,' Pa Otutu said, 'I would hope you wouldn't be here otherwise. Needless for me to say it is a very grand house, and in recent years I have divided the rear segments into flats as my children have moved away. In total there are currently three, four-bedroom, flats. The main house still has eight bedrooms and four toilets, and you can see the compound is very large. If not that I wanted to move away to settle in the village soon, I would have been selling it for much higher than fifty million naira. In fact, more in the region of eighty million naira.'

'I agree with you, it is a very massive compound, and I can see there is much potential.' Yakubu continued, 'However, I have thirty-five million naira that I can transfer to your bank account straightaway and you can have six months to move to your new house. What do you say? Remember a house is only worth what people are willing to pay for it.'

'Ah ah! Mr Yakubu, you cannot enter my house to come and rob me. Eh! I will not allow it!' Otutu erupted.

Mr Yakubu, taken aback, retreated slightly. 'The most I can afford is forty million, and I will have to pay it in instalments.'

Pa Otutu started laughing; a gregarious laugh that filled the veranda. 'It is alright,' Pa Otutu boomed, 'we are still on good terms. If not that I was looking to make a quick sale, I would not be selling to you at this price. I'll take it, what will be the payment plan?'

'I will pay fifteen million naira upfront, pay another fifteen million in six months, then will give you the balance of ten million when you move out.'

'That's OK, but you will pay the balance before I move out, that way I make sure I get my money before I relinquish my house. My son will take you around before you leave.'

Both men got up and shook hands, and Pa Otutu escorted Mr Yakubu to the ground floor. Ben took Mr Yakubu on a quick tour of the house and compound, then they returned to the front of the house. Pa Otutu watched him as he got into his car. He got a sense that this Mr Yakubu was a crafty man. Well, one thing was for sure as far as Pa Otutu was concerned, he wasn't a man to be trifled with. He always came out on top in any battle of wits; a very intelligent and witty man.

The driver got up from the bench he had been sitting on, strode towards the car, got in and started to reverse the car towards the gate. Ben appeared from somewhere and opened the gate as the driver reversed out. Ben closed the gate and walked up to Pa Otutu. 'So how did it go?'

'*Omo me* (my child), we are going to Kokori next week.' Times had changed a bit for Pa Otutu; he was six feet one, wide shoulders, very robust. In the last ten years he was found to be diabetic, and he had been on insulin for the last four years which he took infrequently, depending on how many funds were available. Four years ago, he had also started to lose his vision. He was found to have glaucoma, and it was so bad he had surgery to the right eye a year ago and was scheduled for surgery to the left eye in a few months. In Nigeria there was no timetable, and it was basically when you could afford to pay for healthcare.

This was the reason why he was taking Ben along with him, Ben would be his eyes, and in a strange way he loved having him around. They had always argued, even had physical fights, but as much as he was frustrated by the lack of progress Ben made in his life, secretly a part of him wanted Ben to always be in the house. Even in the distant past when Ben would leave either after a fight, or after he reportedly got himself some form of job, he would always return a few months later.

Pa Otutu continued walking into the house. 'Why don't you cook something for lunch, Ben. My new girlfriend is away at the moment, and she will be back next week.'

'Daddy, you are not serious? At your age, we don't know what charm you are using that you're having more girls than guys who are in their twenties are capable of.'

Chapter Two

Twenty-seven months ago

An incredulous amount of noise could be heard from the Otutu compound in 'Mile Twelve'. Passers-by wondered what was going on; this was more out of curiosity than concern. In truth there was rarely need for concern in most situations. It was just Nigerians were generally exuberant and loud; no place was this stigma truer than in Lagos. Everything ran fast, everything was loud; there was an unapologetic brashness in the air. You either wised up or you would be taken advantage of or worse, pitied.

There was no worse thing than being pitied in a place where most people didn't have enough. People talked about you not only behind your back, but also to your face. Although they might not be that much richer than you, they at least had their pride. If you were robbed, the answer would be 'o sorry o!' Not a sincere emotional expression, but more a sort of 'poor you'. If you were openly proud and some minor disaster befell you, the response would be 'good for you!'; to mean, "you deserved it".

Visible from the streets, Ben was in the upper veranda holding onto his shirt, while ducking simultaneously was

Modupe. Her head was buried in between her hands, and she held Ben's T-shirt with both hands. 'You go kill me today, I'm here and I'm not going anywhere!'

Modupe was Pa Otutu's girlfriend, and she was also the daughter of his ex-concubine who died six months ago. Ben was tall like his father, six feet two, but he wasn't robust, rather he was wiry in appearance, with his limbs covered with tight muscle sinews.

'*U no well, we onieda*, (You are crazy! You must be a witch!),' Ben growled in a mixture of pidgin and Urhobo. 'How can you take the water I fetched and boiled and use it to bath? You know this last two days NEPA has taken light, so the borehole hasn't been pumping water and the tank was empty this morning. Why didn't you go and fetch your own water?'

Boreholes were commonplace in Nigeria; they were a mechanism for drilling for water in the ground, then pumping it into a storage tank for later use. Some people attached the pumping mechanism to already dug wells.

NEPA stood for 'Nigerian Electrical Power Authority': they had been disbanded a few years earlier, but people still referred to whoever was in charge of Nigerian electricity as NEPA. Nothing had changed, in Lagos it was always a variable number of hours of light followed by 'lights out' for a variable number of days or weeks, sometimes even months. Nigerians knew to 'never expect power always'.

'So, is that why you think you could come upstairs and start shouting at me?' Modupe retorted. Ben snarled his mouth and spat out his words, 'You are a *mammiwater* (water mermaid), so you've just come from your meeting with your witches last night. And you planned to come and kill me, after your mother conspired with my dad to kill my mother. Now your mother is dead, you have come here to come and kill me? Chai it will not work o!'

'It is you that is wizard, and your mother a witch,' Modupe retorted. 'Her witchcraft killed her.'

'What!' Ben bellowed, 'Say my mum's name again and I'll slap you, and I promise you, you won't wake up.' Modupe started screaming, and Ben shoved her to the floor, at which she screamed louder and threw in some heavy weeping for more dramatic effect.

From deep within his room, not far from the veranda, Pa Otutu's voice bellowed, 'Ben, you have started.' His heavy footsteps could be heard as he pounded his way from the bedroom to the veranda. Pa Otutu squared off against Ben. 'Ben! Ben! Ben! How many times have I called your name? Eh, my name is not Otutu if I don't kill you today.'

'Old man, go and sit down,' Ben barked. Although his bark was several decibels below Pa Otutu's boom, his bark had a certain sharpness to it that usually put fear into his opponents. This was not the case with Pa Otutu.

'*Mewe*? (is it me?) you are talking?' Pa Otutu shouted while beating his chest. 'Today, today you're leaving this house, go to your own house, and don't come back to mine.'

For those looking from downstairs, this standoff looked like a standoff between an orangutan and a chimpanzee, obviously with Pa Otutu being the orangutan. And so, they argued back and forth for a few more minutes. Until Ben finally pushed his way past Pa Otutu. 'I'm getting out of here, I need to go and clear my head.'

As Ben walked downstairs and out of the compound, Pa Otutu hurled insults at him, even leaning over the veranda as he was leaving the gate, 'Beast of no gender,' he shouted as a parting shot.

'Old man, I'm only going out, I'll be back. If you think I'm moving out of this house, you are mistaken: I'm in my father's house, you go to your own father's house,' Ben retorted as he retreated down the street.

Pa Otutu reached down and lifted Modupe to her feet. 'Sorry, dear,' he said. 'You won't see him again.' She came to Pa Otutu's side and joined in hurling insults, with her voice growing louder and her animations becoming more agitated the further Ben got towards the end of the streets. She had her hands in the air, then around her waist, then she untied her wrapper (brightly printed cloth) making as if to go after Ben, as Pa Otutu held her back.

Modupe had only moved her things into the house for the last one month. Pa Otutu's children were not happy about it. It was after this that it became apparent that Pa Otutu was now dating the daughter of his previous mistress, who had died about six months ago. The rumour was that he was sleeping with both of them; even while the mum was alive. When her mother was alive, she had only visited the house once. But since her mother died, she initially made sporadic visits on the pretence of picking something up or bringing up some food for Pa Otutu. The visits became more frequent, resulting in overnight stays, then she moved in a month ago.

Pa Otutu's children were not around frequently and on the off chance they saw her visiting the house, they had assumed that she was visiting out of gratitude that her mum was treated well by Pa Otutu. Only in the last two months did suspicions arise when she started staying over some nights, and a month ago she came with a taxi with some of her stuff, then she disappeared for a day and then returned another day with more of her things.

Reports of these happenings in Mile Twelve had even spread overseas. Kevwe had called Ogaga to relate Pa Otutu's behaviour and why his children were becoming more distant from him, and he had also fed Ogaga some disturbing news. Or rather, what they perceived to be disturbing news. He informed Ogaga that Pa Otutu was intent on selling the house and moving back to the village. He apparently hadn't consulted any of the children and not left any contingencies in place for his children.

This made the children feel that Pa Otutu was taking deliberate actions to actually hurt them. All twenty something of his children were born in Lagos, and they grew up in Lagos. Where would they live? At present Ben and the two youngest children still lived in the house.

On a deeper note, the children of his first wife were really hurt. They felt Pa Otutu had contributed directly to her death some four years ago. She had worked tirelessly to feed the family and look after Pa Otutu. All Pa Otutu rewarded her with was suffering. He brought in another woman, a year before her death, who happened to be the mother of his current mistress.

Then there were many fights, with Pa Otutu taking the side of his mistress. He had been physically abusive to his first wife, he had neglected looking after her children, and he insulted her relentlessly. In spite of this, all his first wife did in return was to respect him, show him love, cook for him and give him the little money she made from her trade, hoping that perhaps the heart of this man who had once loved her would melt.

It did not. About a fortnight before her death, there was an altercation that involved Pa Otutu, his mistress, his first wife and Ben. The mistress had started insulting Ben's mum, and obviously Ben intervened, and Otutu took the side of the mistress. There was a ferocious argument in the upper living space of Pa Otutu's room. It got so violent that Ben's mum tried to restrain Ben.

In the confusion of the moment, the mistress reached into her bosom, pulled her right hand out and lunged for Ben's private part. Ben's mum reacted quickly jumping in the way, but she immediately fell down to the floor and became paralysed. She was neither pushed nor hit, but only touched by the hand of the mistress. The rest of her children came and carried her to her room. It took her a week to recover. After that incident, two weeks later she came home, collapsed and never breathed again.

Chapter Three

Twenty-six months ago

Mr Yakubu had just left the bank, after paying the initial deposit of fifteen million naira into Pa Otutu's Central Bank of Nigeria account. Transferring money this way saved one carrying around bags of cash and made you less attractive to robbers. He walked back into the parking lot and got into his car. The driver had remained seated in the car this time around, as he had opined it would only take his boss a few minutes to sort out his business in the bank. The windows were wound down, it was a very hot day, and the air was very stiff.

The driver switched the car on and put the air conditioning on before winding the windows up. They were back in the blue Toyota Auris, and they were heading back to Mile Twelve. He wasn't going to see Mr Otutu, but he called Mr Otutu on the phone, informing him he had made the initial transfer. Pa Otutu acknowledged that he had received an alert from his bank.

Yakubu's purpose of visit was a little bit more sinister; he was going to meet someone. He had a spy in Agility. Someone he knew. Yakubu wanted to find out all he could about Mr Otutu. This wasn't going to be hard. Mr Otutu was well known in Mile Twelve; he couldn't hide himself even if he tried. Mile Twelve was a small place, and Mr Otutu and his family had lived there for nearly thirty years now. He was known for his womanising way, and once one of his neighbours even tried to attack him with a machete when he learnt Mr Otutu had been with his wife.

Mr Yakubu knew he couldn't force Mr Otutu into doing anything, but he felt he didn't have to pay forty million naira; he had paid fifteen million so far. He intended to pay only twenty million of the agreed fee. The fifteen million he had already paid to Mr Otutu and five million to this lady he was about to meet. Her name was Modupe, and when he learnt of her he couldn't pass on this opportunity.

Mr Yakubu was a businessman; his strong point was blackmail and manipulation. Blackmail wasn't an option with Mr Otutu, it would be manipulation. For the last four months since his first visit to Mile Twelve, he had thought of ways in which he could get hold of Mr Otutu's house. He had forty million in the bank, but that was the sum of all he had in the bank. Things also had changed a bit, as he wasn't getting as many kickbacks as he used to. Unfortunately, his contact in the government who used to award him contracts had suddenly passed away a few months ago from a heart attack. This was before he had packed up the syndicate, otherwise he would have continued his work with the syndicate.

So, this house was insurance for the future and his pension plan. His mistress would be grateful for it and raise his son properly, and the other rooms in the house he would rent. The house was his, only Mr Otutu didn't know it yet.

When he heard of Mr Otutu's relationship with Modupe, he was glad! This might just be the opportunity he was looking for; a chance to get eyes on Mr Otutu's house and a controlling hand on his heart. He met Modupe as she was going home from one of her visits to Mr Otutu's house. As in his traditional manner, he had been stalking the street where she arrived. He parked about a street away from her house, pretending to mind his own business, as she came round the corner.

He knew she was his mistress. He stopped her initially, pretending he wanted some directions. 'Young lady, could you direct me to Mr Otutu's house? I'm trying to find Bisi Street.'

'Hey, *Oga*, you cannot be serious, I'm just coming from there,' Modupe answered him.

This was how their conversation began. He invited her into the car, volunteering to take her home if she would be his guide. In the car he relayed that actually he wanted to give her some money because she was so helpful and such a beautiful girl, all twenty-eight years of her. He asked for her number so he could call her every time he came. He gave a few thousand nairas and was rewarded with a phone number.

He was right, she was a woman that could be bought with money. Probably explains why she is with Mr Otutu, she is probably after the house herself Yakubu thought to himself. Modupe was indeed a fine girl. All five feet five inches of her, with her big *derrière* and hourglass figure. These were slightly disguised by her uncultured ways and the shapeless clothes she wore. If he had not had his eye on the house, his eye would now be on Modupe.

After they got to the gate, he made the excuse that he was only coming to see the place as he was due to be visiting next week with some business friends, so just wanted to work out the location. His driver turned the car around and they proceeded to drop her home.

Over the next few weeks he visited her frequently at her house. He had figured her out as an opportunist. He promised her lots of money; he was sure more than she had ever seen in her life. Five million naira to a young lady who had no income and was sleeping with a man in his late sixties for rewards of small amounts of money. If she would go through with his plan, her future would be guaranteed.

The plan was made, Modupe would move in with Mr Otutu; there she would gain a controlling hand in the house and hasten his move out of the house. If he was happy to move early to Kokori, that would be fine. If not, she would have to hasten his departure from this life. As Modupe flared up in alarm at the mention of this, Yakubu was sure it wasn't out of concern about the morality of what was suggested or care for Mr Otutu. It was out of concern about what she had to do.

'You have to earn your money,' Mr Yakubu would say. The purpose of her being in the house would be twofold; firstly, to get him the deeds for the house; secondly to hasten his departure. Only on completion of these tasks would he get her five million naira. In the meantime, he would pay all her expenses.

Modupe sat and thought for a while, then getting up she exclaimed, 'I have a solution! I know a powerful herbalist. He would give me some charm so Otutu will do whatever I ask him to do. He will give me the deeds and he will move out of the house one way or another. Just understand you have to give this time. If it happens too quickly people will be suspicious, give me six to nine months.'

Mr Yakubu was prepared to wait; he could play the long game. After all, this was about his pension, and at present money wasn't too much of a problem for him. He left her house, leaving her with a wad of twenty-thousand-naira notes to encourage her.

The plan had been made; the wheels had been set in motion. Mr Yakubu was very sure about her before he approached her. He kept on asking himself the question: so her mother lived with Mr Otutu for three years, 'What kind of person starts an affair with her mother's lover?'

Chapter Four

Twenty-four months ago

Sitting on the upper veranda was Pa Otutu; he had made up his mind. For the last few years he had been longing for home. This house in Mile Twelve had been home for him and his family for nearly thirty years. Prior to that they had lived near Anthony.

The house was feeling empty, and Pa Otutu felt this was probably because he missed a family. His last wife had left three years ago; his first wife had died about six years ago. Most of his children had moved away, and it was just Ben and Ochuko that were around; Irhorho came to visit from time to time. And sometimes he would see Efe.

It never occurred to Pa Otutu that his desire to belong somewhere and be with valued people might lie with his numerous children. But rather he thought of the village and his kinsmen. He thought it would be a good idea if he went back to where he grew up, and where he would be appreciated, especially with the house he was building and with the money he would have when the sale of his property was complete.

'Ben, I'm going to Kokori, we need to see how far the building has come,' Pa Otutu said. 'You know the last time we went, we tore down the old building; since then we've done the foundation, and we are looking to raise the building to roofing level. I'll need you to accompany me there.'

'No problem, Dad, you just have to give me a few days' notice of when you are ready to go,' Ben said. 'Will we be taking the new car you bought? I have to tell you it is a very nice ride!' Ben said, beaming.

'What is a ride?' Otutu asked.

'Your car. I will have to take it for a drive one of these days,' Ben said.

'Over my dead body. Nobody is driving my car apart from my driver. Just remember that if I catch you!'

'Dad, you can't be like that. You know it will be nice for me to get myself around sometimes. Besides if I took it out you probably wouldn't know.'

Pa Otutu had bought a new car since he had the initial fifteen million deposited in his account. He had spent four million naira on the black and white Peugeot, it was a lovely car. He had so far spent four million on doing the foundation, and a further two million naira on raising the walls of the house. Pa Otutu was excited about bringing the house to roofing level.

'Well. I've said what I've got to say,' Pa Otutu remonstrated, opening his palms out wide and then placing them on his lap. 'Just be ready for Monday next week; we will be leaving first thing in the morning. You know how the road is to Delta state. I have to get things done quickly. I want to move home as soon as possible, even my new girlfriend wants to come and stay; she is actually encouraging me to go.'

Ben sighed… 'Well, Daddy, that is something I want to talk to you about. Are you sure about that woman? She is dangerous, I'm sure of it. I'm really scared for you; seeing that of all the wives that you've married, none of them are left. And now we have this nobody, who has come to inherit where she did not labour.'

'Ben, be careful, be very careful...' Otutu started to say.

'Daddy, wait,' Ben continued; 'ever since she has moved into this house you are different. It's like you leave so much to her. You give her money to go shopping, you leave her to cook, you even tell her things that I wouldn't expect you to tell her. And it looks like with her being here she is looking after you, but you are not looking like you are looked after. Especially in this last month. You have lost weight, and you are sleeping more than normal. When a man is with a woman and he doesn't look well, there is something wrong!'

'Ben, I think I've heard enough,' Otutu sighed. 'I know you are much older than her and that is what is bothering you. You want her for yourself, is it not so?'

'Abomination, Daddy, you know the ladies chase after me. Why would I want a witch? Anyway, before we both get upset, I'll stop talking about her but, Daddy, I've warned you.' Ben finished on this note, wagging his finger vigorously in Otutu's face.

Otutu looked down at his chest, 'Ben, go and do whatever you were doing before.' He kept his gaze to the floor as Ben walked away. He heard Ben rapping as he walked down the long hallway from the upper veranda.

'The moonlight beamed off the sea's blue face. Her face was so mean, it was green, and so the thing goes, when evil thought she had a chance...'

As Ben walked down the dark corridor, he felt his father had become more docile recently, like he was being controlled.

Even just speaking to him a few minutes ago, normally he would have erupted in shouting bouts. The man who no one could control, and in certain ways couldn't control himself when it came to women, seemed a bit subdued in his eyes.

It wasn't until a few days later that he became even more afraid; he could swear that on that evening while walking past the kitchen, he saw Modupe slip something from her wrapper into the soup. It wasn't from the salt or pepper container; it was from a little nylon she had hidden in her wrapper.

He found himself becoming more and more cautious of Modupe as the days and weeks wore on. Not just because of that incident, but there were times that he would witness his father being calm and a bit indifferent for long periods of time, then at a different hour of the day he would become his normal gregarious self. Singing, calling him for no particular reason at all, just to get his attention, and talking proudly about himself and his achievements.

He would talk aloud that he had educated his children; he sent two of his sons to London and they were doing well. Ogaga was a medical doctor, and Ruemu was a successful businessman. Even in Australia, Ufuoma was doing great, and he would go on and on about how all his children were doing well.

It seemed to Ben as if during these episodes, he had temporarily been released from under some sort of control, and this was manifested by an explosion of his personality; if this was possible, that one's personality could be caged in only for it to temporarily escape its jail until a door was shut on it again.

Ben had made his mind up; he would be calling a meeting with the other older children. He needed to speak to Ese, Onajevwe, Kevwe; in fact, he would even call Mute who had only just travelled to America. At least things were getting better now two of his mother's children were now overseas. First Choja went to London, now Mute was in America.

Chapter Five

Old boys' club

The boys had gathered together; they met in a beer parlour, near Kevwe's house in Ikorodu. Ben wanted to keep this meeting as far away from the house as possible. Seated around the table were Ben, Kevwe and Ese.

'Guys, eh, mm… You know that new woman that Daddy has is a witch, *Onyi Onieda* . She is trying to kill him, honestly, I'm very worried. The old man hasn't been the same for the last two months. He seems so docile and he bends to her every will. He doesn't argue with her, sometimes it is like he is in some kind of stupor,' Ben began to say.

'I think she has cast a spell on him. In the last few days, he is in his room for hours on end, he doesn't come out. We have all had our issues with Dad, but this matter affects all of us. I think she is after the house and the new-found money the old man has come into.'

'What are you saying?' Ese asked. 'I saw Daddy a few months ago, but in that case I need to go and visit him.'

Kevwe then chirped in, 'I think that is a good idea. We all know the old man can be irrational when it comes to women, but we have never worried about his safety before. Ese, I'll come with you.'

Ese then continued, 'I think we should tell Onajevwe to move back to Daddy's house. She is renting elsewhere and cannot afford her rent. If she moved back, it would be good for her and she can help to look after the old man and, you know, as a woman, cook for him.

'She can also make sure he isn't being poisoned, and he is looking after himself. Ever since I've left for Jos due to my filming schedule six months ago, Onajevwe has had to fend for herself and her children, as she couldn't stay with me anymore.'

'I think that's an excellent idea,' Ben said. 'Let us do that. I want you guys to see him today, and I'm sure when you see him, you will agree with me that something needs to change. That woman cannot stay in the house, she must be removed.'

Kevwe suddenly burst out in laughter, pointing a finger at Ben's face. 'Can you see your face? It looks like you are scared of that young girl.'

'Kevwe, I won't even lie to you, I'm scared. I've seen a lot of things in life, been through hell, but something tells me that there is another power at work behind that woman. If you see the boldness with which she walks around the house; from the outside she appears to be serving Daddy, but she is doing something else to him. As small as she is, she is so aggressive.'

Kevwe then said, 'Ben, you shouldn't talk like that. You know as a Christian whatever charm she might have shouldn't affect you.'

To which Ben replied, 'I know, but there is just something about her...'

His voice trailed away as he gazed at the traffic that flew by in front of the restaurant.

Ben was lost in his thoughts; in recent weeks he had taken to locking his bedroom doors and even making sure the window nettings were on at night time. He felt there was a new presence in the house, something foreign. Every home had its issues; the arrival of Modupe had brought with it a trainload of negative connotations.

Ese got up. 'Thank you, Ben. Kevwe, let's go, we have no time to lose.' Ben and Kevwe also got up, and as if in tandem they all picked up their bottles of minerals and swigged down the remainder till each bottle was empty and they walked out of the restaurant just as they had walked in. Kevwe left three hundred naira notes on the table, secured underneath an empty bottle, for the waiter to pick up.

They hopped on a *Kekenapeg (a tripod motorcade)*, often abbreviated to *Keke* and told the driver to head to Mile Twelve.

At the Gate

As the *Kekenapeg* pulled up in front of the house twenty minutes after the brothers had boarded it, they saw a blue Toyota driving away. 'That's the car of the man that wants to buy the house. Ah what is he doing here? I don't remember Daddy inviting him,' Ben said.

'Look there, it looks like he was talking to Modupe,' said Kevwe, pointing at the light-framed lady with the big buttocks entering into their father's compound. She entered and remained in front of the lower veranda with her arms folded in front of her, shuffling her feet impatiently.

They hopped off the *Keke*. Kevwe delved into his back pocket, brought out his wallet and gave five hundred naira to the driver; it was how much they had promised him to bring them this far; *Kekes* were more suited to doing shorter journeys, but the brothers figured it would be quicker than a taxi.

The brothers, Ese, Ben and Kevwe, went into the compound. 'Good afternoon,' they greeted Modupe, at which she kissed her teeth.

'Ttwmmm… what is good about the afternoon? And what are all of you doing here?'

'Are you mad?' Ben said, putting his right index finger to his right temple; he then broke into pidgin English, *'Abi something dey worry you,* (something must be wrong with you).' She kissed her teeth again, looking away from them.

It was then that they realised she was positioned right in the middle of the entrance to the ground floor veranda, which was the entrance to the house. Ben started to move towards her, and Ese quickened his stride and guided Ben around her and they walked around her into the house. Kevwe paused as he came up beside her, 'I don't know what is wrong with you, but we have come to see our father, and you should show more respect. Everyone here is older than you.'

He paused again as he went past her, 'You know if anyone of us slapped you, you would die!'

She roared, *'Abeg commot for my face,* (get out of my sight). Older or whatever you call yourself, you are all baboons. Besides nobody is seeing Daddy today, he is sleeping. He told me to make sure nobody disturbs him.' Kevwe gritted his teeth, shook his head and walked in. He thought to himself that if only she was a man, he would have taken out her two front teeth, and they would have beaten her silly.

As they walked into the house, in came Onajevwe through the gate. She had just alighted from an *Ocada* (motorbike). She walked straight in and immediately sensed the tension in the atmosphere. She ignored Modupe.

Modupe was standing where she was because she contemplated what she needed to do. She had just met with Yakubu, and he had told her to hurry up the proceedings, he couldn't wait any longer. He had already paid fifteen million naira to Otutu, and as he had said before, he would rather give her two million naira, than give Mr Otutu any more money. Modupe had been daily adding a small amount of a potion she had got from the herbalist to Pa Otutu's food over the last few weeks. The fee had come down from five million to two million because of the amount of time this was taking. Mr Yakubu had repeatedly told her, time is money, get to work.

Pa Otutu had finally started to succumb to her methods. This was a critical time; she couldn't let things go wrong at this stage, she had worked too hard. She turned around and hurried after them. She had no idea how to play this, but do something she would, before the fee dropped to five hundred thousand naira! She shrugged her shoulders in horror as she imagined this.

The men and Onajevwe had entered into Pa Otutu's living space upstairs. They turned left to where the bedroom was. As Ben led the way, he tried knocking. 'Daddy, it's me, are you there?' he asked.

There was a faint answer. 'I'm OK, are you there?'

Ben tried to push the door open, but found it was locked. He kept jerking the door handle and pushing harder, not registering that the door was locked. 'It is locked,' Kevwe said. They turned around to face Modupe, who had her hands on her hips and a nonchalant look on her face.

'Where is the key?' they all asked in unison. 'Come on

and open the door.'

She looked at them, unwrapped the key from her wrapper around her waist, then dropped it between her breasts. 'Nobody is opening this door today but me. I've been looking after your father all this time and you think you can just barge in here. You better find your way out of here.'

Onajevwe lunged at her. Ese stepped in and restrained her. 'Not now, not here,' he said. A huge fracas broke out, and a heated exchange erupted between Modupe and the children in the living space just outside the bedroom.

'Look at this antelope,' Onajevwe said. 'So you think this is a jungle where you can do as you please. If not for God, I would have dealt with you in this place.'

Through all of this commotion, Pa Otutu didn't make any attempt to come out and, more strangely, he didn't utter a word. Ese brought an end to the argument after about ten minutes of back and forth. 'Well, it looks like you have bewitched him, lucky for you we are decent people. Because you are a woman we'll leave you alone, but you don't understand that we are children of God, and no amount of witchcraft can do anything to us.'

'Let us go!' Ese said, turning to his siblings, and they turned and followed. Ben was still confused by this and was the last to turn and follow. As they got downstairs, Ese said, 'We have to do this properly and do it tonight. We are going to the police station and we will get her arrested. This is forced imprisonment and we have to do something before it gets out of hand.'

'You are very wise,' Kevwe said. 'If we did anything to her, we could be on the wrong side of the law, and we won't be able to get her out of the house.'

So the siblings came out of the compound, hailed a taxi and were on their way to the police station in Mile Twelve.

The Officers

At eight pm exactly, four police officers, all clad in black, followed the children into the compound. They went upstairs with the torches of the officers leading the way because there was no light. The children had spent four good hours at the station before the officers were convinced to come.

They knew the officers could have made that decision in ten minutes if they had just given them a wad of cash. That wasn't a luxury the children could afford. Instead they spoke to about three different ranking officers. Each of them gave a written statement, and then the commissioner decided—after going for dinner at home and coming back—that it was a case worth pursuing. They set off an hour after they had made this decision.

They ran into Modupe as they came into the top veranda. She had seen them from the top veranda, and she had now taken up her position outside Pa Otutu's door. 'Madam,' said a female officer. 'We have come to see Pa Otutu and check what state he is in, as we are suspicious of some form of abuse.'

'Don't speak any grammar to me, you stupid woman,' Modupe said in response. The officer then asked for the key, to which Modupe replied, 'I don't know where it is, I'm standing outside because I can't find it.' As the officer started to warn Modupe about her failure to co-operate, she lunged at her and started raining blows on her. The other three officers— one other woman and two men—stepped in, picking her off the female officer and restraining her, then Modupe started crying.

She was handcuffed while one of the male officers—tired of the delay and thinking he needed to go home for dinner—kicked the door down with his boot.

There lay Pa Otutu, with drool down the side of his mouth. Half-naked except for a wrapper around his waist, and when the light flashed on the bed, it looked like he had been doubly incontinent—he had not been able to go to the loo. At first, they were not sure if he was alive, but he was making respiratory effort on closer inspection.

Each of the children filed into the room, even Modupe followed them with her hands cuffed behind her back. Ese and Ben quickly crouched down slapping his cheeks, to which Pa Otutu responded with a low moan.

The officers jumped on Modupe and started beating her. The brothers picked up their father and started making their way out of the room and downstairs. The beating stopped as Pa Otutu was moved and, although one female officer kept her arm in the crook of Modupe's arm, the others helped to carry Pa Otutu downstairs. They took them to the taxi stand in Mile Twelve and advised them to take Pa Otutu to the hospital as soon as possible, and at least one of them to report to the station in the morning.

Chapter Six

Twenty months ago

'We live today, but yesterday never goes away. If you have lived once, could you some day, cease to exist'.

Lying on his hospital bed at Badagry military hospital was Pa Otutu. He faced away from the door in a surgical ward full of about twenty-four patients; he had been placed in a surgical ward because there was no space on the medical ward. All lying on single beds, the mattresses were pretty much mostly identical: a slim piece of brown foam with multiple stains on them which only added character to the mattresses. Some of the mattresses smelt of urine. The men that sat or lay on these mattresses seemed quite disinterested in their environment and smelt also of urine besides other bodily waste smells. Gosh, there wasn't much to look at. The identical mattresses were set on a low-set black spring bed, reminiscent of the bed that Ogaga slept on in his father's house when he was a child.

The combination of this piece of mattress on the black spring bed led to the situation where you could feel the springs right under your skin, and every movement resulted in you bouncing. You had to be careful not to catch a toe or finger at the points where the coils of springs inserted into the hooks in the black frame. These points were at the edges of the bed.

Only the plastered brick wall and glass windows seemed to have been constructed properly. Through which they could see the heads of the nurses and their white caps in their offices. The nurses didn't look interested either; they seemed to move in a very slow disordered rhythm with no purpose in ends, responding after several minutes to the calls of the patients, or the view of the dull fat nurse pushing the drugs trolley along doing her drugs round. Ogaga thought that it seemed nurses throughout Western Africa were the same, they tended to move in that slow manner, lacking any purpose or determination. They laboured to answer questions or carry out tasks, with mundane requests easily exhausting ten minutes to find out a question like say, 'where is my father?'

There was a nurse at the desk at the entrance to the ward: she seemed more irritated than disinterested. A young man in traditional attire had come up to the main desk; he looked dishevelled, his hair was short and uncombed, and his cloth clung to his body, most likely from sweating in the Nigerian heat. He carried a leather bag in his hand and was dragging a black and blue travelling box. He wore a brown top and bottom with flowered patterns all over it; the top was one of the three-quarter-arm length outfits commonly worn among younger Urhobo men. 'Hello,' he said, in what she could imagine was a British accent. 'I've come to see Pa Otutu, he is my father.'

'I haven't seen you before. Have you come before?' she said, as a curious scowl came across her face.

Ogaga said, 'I've just come off the plane. I live in London so that's why you haven't seen me. How is he doing?'

'Well, he is OK, he is taking his medications and he really doesn't need to be here,' mused the nurse. 'He should be going home.'

'What is wrong with him and what treatment has he had?'

'Well, in his notes he has had some medications and fluids,' the nurse replied. A bewildered look came over the young man. He thought to himself what kind of answer is 'he has had medication and fluids'.

He found this very amusing, as he was a doctor himself. Never could he imagine that this would be his communication to relatives or even the nurse's communications to relatives back in the UK. He could just imagine the conversation; 'Excuse me! My mum is in here after being brought in by ambulance a week ago. How is she?'

'Well, she has had some fluids and medications according to the notes.'

It certainly wouldn't happen in England. That nurse probably wouldn't last long in his or her job if he or she were that clueless. After ascertaining that the visiting individual was actually a relative, a lengthy conversation would probably follow explaining how the patient was and giving a diagnosis and the current management plan—very specific details being omitted as most relatives mostly do not need to know about it.

Trying to be as nice as possible, Ogaga persevered with the nurse, who was used to working in a health system that was unresponsive to people's needs and, more significantly, unaccountable to anybody. This was, in a way, a summation of many government organisations. The government of Nigeria is guilty of the charges of being both unresponsive because it does not care and unaccountable because it doesn't know what it means to have law.

'Can I read his notes please? I'm a doctor in the UK,' at which the woman beamed from one side of her wide face to the other.

'Oh!' she exclaimed.

Sometimes admitting you were a doctor in Nigeria gave you a certain leeway. Perhaps the leeway for people to treat you with the respect and courtesy everyone should be afforded in the first place. Ogaga remembered his last trip to Nigeria, where he was called over to the side by one of the customs officers, who was pretending to make enquiry into who he was and where he was going. The customs officer was intuitively looking for a bribe. Ogaga had made up his mind a long time ago not to give bribes; he felt it fed the status quo. His attitude was that it is not my fault things are hard, and by giving bribes I'm just exacerbating the situation and making it harder for everyone. You keep allowing your boss not to pay you because you found an alternative in getting bribes from travellers.

The customs officer came across his name on his British passport, which had doctor prefixing his first. Then he asked 'What do you do?'

Ogaga replied, 'I'm a doctor.'

'A medical doctor?' the customs officer asked.

'Yes, I am,' Ogaga replied.

The frown disappeared from the customs officer's face; he handed the passports back to Ogaga and said, with a wry smile, 'have a safe trip'. Before he became a doctor, Ogaga would have probably ended up quarrelling with him till the officer realised he wasn't getting anything from him. Ogaga had in the past sat in the customs office at Murtala Muhammed airport for this same reason, as various officers tried to exert pressure on him to extract bribes.

Pa Otutu's medical record read like a rap sheet: uncontrolled diabetes, high blood pressure, delusions—which was a way of saying he was having hallucinations. The report also suggested a urinary tract infection, 'infection of unknown origin', collapse and so his records read. He was on a myriad of tablets. He was even on quetiapine, which is a very strong tranquiliser used to sedate patients and treat serious psychotic symptoms. The reason this had been started Ogaga couldn't begin to understand. He looked through the record, looked through his investigations to date and examined the plans. The last entries all suggested that he was medically ready for discharge, and perhaps he might benefit from an outpatient CT scan of his head to investigate some putative psychotic symptoms. These said psychotic symptoms only seemed to appear when Pa Otutu wanted them to.

During his inpatient stay, they restarted his high blood pressure and diabetic medications. His blood pressure and sugar levels returned to normal levels within that time. The doctors, however, noted that he appeared to be experiencing visual hallucinations at times and acting irrationally, for example chasing the female nurses around the ward, touching their bums and breasts, and from time to time defaecating on himself or wetting himself, and then appearing to talk out loud without talking to anyone in particular. Ogaga wondered how much of this was truly psychotic for a man who had over twenty-five known children, married six wives besides concubines and girlfriends and probably in his heart of hearts just loved women.

He was known to love being the centre of attraction and some of his children would argue that this wasn't new behaviour and in the past, from time to time, had done dramatic things, such as rolling around crying on the floor after a loss, defaecating on himself when he was possibly unwell and expecting his youngest son to clean up after him. One thing was right, he loved to be the centre of attention, whether as a lady's man or as a patient needing your undivided attention.

Ogaga thought it was difficult to always work out which symptoms were purely cultural, such as rolling on the floor and wailing loudly in times of tragedy, which seemed to generally be a West African cultural norm for many people. Ogaga had seen behaviours like this with his patients; he remembered a lady he saw who came in to see him with left-sided abdominal pain and fever: she was a sickle cell carrier. During the consultation she had an attack of pain and started screaming and rolling around; at a point she stopped and started taking deep breaths. Ogaga was so moved that he called for the crash trolley and his colleagues to help him. After they had flustered around her, he called an ambulance which took her to the hospital.

It turned out she had a kidney infection, which had resulted in a crisis even though she was a sickle cell carrier. She was discharged home three days later after being treated with intravenous antibiotics.

The nurse pointed to a bed behind her and to her left. The young man walked up to Pa Otutu, who was sitting up with his legs on the floor and hunched over as if he was sitting on a stool. He came around to the front and greeted Pa Otutu (in the traditional greeting), smiling, 'Daddy *Miguo*.' The greeting literally meant 'I'm on my knees'.

Pa Otutu exclaimed, 'Ese, is it you?'

'No, Dad, it is me, Ogaga.' He couldn't blame him; after all, they were brothers.

'Ogaga!' he exclaimed, and then started crying. 'Look at

me! I've been meaning to speak to you and your brother Ruemu, but no one has helped me.'

Ogaga replied, 'But I spoke to you three weeks ago. After that, every time I tried to speak to you no one picked up your phone.' Ogaga remembered the last phone call he had made from London: his dad had picked up but sounded drowsy and distant; he had then handed the phone over to the mistress who ended the call.

Still crying and sputtering, he cried, 'My child, my child, look at my state.'

'It is alright, Dad, I'm sorry I couldn't come earlier, but it is good to see you now. Tell me what has happened.'

'They tried to kill me, but we thank God they didn't succeed. Well, it is Ben and Ese that have been looking after me since I've been here.'

He sat on the chair beside his bed and they talked. He also presented Pa Otutu with a shirt he had bought for him; the customary bottle of gin he kept in his bag, as Pa Otutu was in no state to be drinking. In Urhobo culture every memorable event, personal or corporate, involved alcohol. Even with events as small as paying someone a visit, a bottle of schnapps was opened and some kolanut broken and eaten; it was a sign of good fellowship.

In his father's house, this would have been followed by his dad bringing out some soft drinks. Blessing the drinks, breaking the kolanut and whoever was present sharing in the kolanut and drinks. After that, Ogaga would have presented his gifts, and his dad would have prayed for him.

'My son, how is your surgery. Which surgery are you doing now?'

'Dad, I'm a GP.'

'What is that?' Pa Otutu enquired.

'Well, a general practitioner, essentially a family doctor.'

Pa Otutu continued, 'My son, remember you must be a surgeon. Come and I'll build a hospital here in Nigeria, in Warri. It will be very big and you would do very well, then you can give me some money. I'm telling you will give me money and nobody else.'

'Yes, Dad, I will,' Ogaga said with a wry smile. Knowing it wasn't going to happen but knowing that Pa Otutu would not understand nor would it make any difference even if he tried to explain. Ogaga had considered surgery in the past, but he felt it was too competitive, and he wasn't that competitive. Most people assumed because you got into medical school you had to be competitive. Ogaga enjoyed a bit of everything.

'Son, do you know I was building my house in Kokori village?'

'I heard about it,' Ogaga replied.

Pa Otutu continued, 'I was going to move back to the village. I've done the house up to roofing level; I've even bought the furniture for the house. You see if you come to open your hospital in Warri, you will make a lot of money, and you will give me some. You will give only to me. I'm not talking about the rest of your brothers.'

This was the second time Pa Otutu was going on about only him receiving money from Ogaga. Ogaga had over the decade helped out some of his siblings financially, paying for their university educations and, much to his annoyance, sending large sums of money for reported emergencies. Once, one of his brothers, Kevwe, was stuck in Dubai. He had travelled there for business. As often occurred when he pursued business ventures, it didn't work out. He was apparently duped and didn't have any money to pay his hotel bills, so he was taken to prison in Dubai. He called Ogaga in London, who had to send money for him to be released and to fly back to Nigeria.

'Daddy, do you want to talk to my fiancée?'

'Let me talk to my daughter.'

So Ogaga picked up his phone and dialled his fiancée, who happened to be spending that week at her parents' house.

'Hi, honey, how are you?'

'I'm fine, baby, how is Nigeria treating you?' she replied.

'Well thank goodness. I'm finally in Lagos, sitting in the hospital with my dad.'

'Oh! Can I speak to him?' she exclaimed.

'Well, that's why I called you, honey.'

He handed the phone over to his father, asking at the same time, 'Would you like to speak to my fiancée?'

'Hello, daughter,' Pa Otutu bellowed. 'What is your name?'

After speaking to her, he spoke to her dad.

'Hello, my in-law. This is your father-in-law,' Ogaga's fiancée's dad said over the phone.

Pa Otutu replied, 'Well, this is your father in-law!' The young couple burst out in laughter in the background. They continued to exchange pleasantries until they said their goodbyes.

He had spoken jovially to her and her father and even prayed for her. After he finished the phone conversation, he turned to Ogaga and said, 'I didn't say anything bad, did I?'

And in like manner they continued in conversation for the next hour. The young man examined him and satisfied himself that there was nothing more he could do medically. He said his goodbyes when his father tired. Ogaga went to find the doctor looking after him to discuss what the problem was with his father and what else needed to be done.

At the doctor's office, he waited an hour to speak to the doctor and even in that wait there were many people in front of him. Ogaga played the doctor card, otherwise he would have been there all day. He didn't find the conversation with his father's overseeing doctor very helpful. After waiting for around fifteen minutes, he knocked on the doctor's door and walked right in. 'Hello, I'm Dr Ogaga, I would like to speak to you about my father.'

She looked at him with a surprised look. The doctor then said, 'Please wait, I'm coming. You see there are a lot of people in front of you.'

'I know,' Ogaga said, 'but there is a problem. I've just arrived on a flight and I need to go back soon. Just wanted to make sure you haven't forgotten me.'

'Go and wait please,' she said in a drawn voice. After waiting another fifteen minutes, he popped his head around again. She again implored him, saying, 'Please give me another five minutes.' If there was one quality about Ogaga, it was that he was persistent.

Standing around in the office there definitely wasn't any privacy or confidentiality. It was the outpatient clinic. There were about eight other patients lined up against the wall, waiting to see one of the two doctors in the room. The two doctors were separated by a blue screen. Everyone in the room could clearly hear all the conversations that were going on in the room. There was some semblance of order, and the waiting patients generally kept quiet except for the occasional moan or complaint. This was probably in gratitude that they were not on the other side of the door in the queue that stretched halfway along the outpatients' corridor. With some patients sitting on the floor, some sitting on long rectangular benches, and others leaning with their backs against the wall.

Ogaga had confidently strutted right through the queue, right up to the door. He didn't look like a patient, and he figured he looked remotely important, and perhaps his greatest tool was that he sounded different. Putting on his best English accent as he walked by patient after patient. 'Excuse me please. Sorry. I beg your pardon,' he said to another. All to good effect as he got to the door, knocked and waltzed right in.

Ogaga didn't question the ethics of his behaviour. This was Nigeria; it is a dog eat dog world. Sadly, he guessed it was actually the same all over the world, just masquerading in different forms. The bottom line remained that an air of privilege bought people certain liberties, and the extent varied depending on which society you were talking about.

Trying to be too proper or adhering too strictly to an order that wasn't shared here in Nigeria is detrimental to your survival. Survival wasn't everything for Ogaga; he believed in honour. As far as he was concerned this was for the health of his father, and he couldn't wait till it got dark while waiting patiently. He recognised the potential dangers in travelling late as a non-resident of his country. Besides he was getting married soon, and Nigeria wasn't a good enough excuse to get out of that engagement.

While he waited, he mused on the stories of dangers he had heard about in the Nigerian health system. One such story was of a 70-year-old man who had collapsed on the day after arriving from the UK. He was still breathing. He was rushed to a private clinic where he was seen by the doctor there. The doctor started him on fluids and treatment for typhoid, and advised his relatives that hopefully he should pick up soon and feel better. Two hours went by and the man didn't improve. It wasn't until the relatives had had enough and took him to another private clinic that the doctor there diagnosed the collapsed gentleman with a stroke.

Poor practice is ubiquitous throughout the Nigerian health systems, but there are a few pockets of good practice. Ogaga wasn't aware of any centres of excellence, so he couldn't write them off yet. He didn't live in Nigeria so he didn't know.

Five minutes later, the said doctor, Dr Ogunsola, called him in. 'OK, Dr Ogaga, how can I help?'

'I understand you are the doctor looking after my father.'

'Yes, I am,' Dr Ogunsola said.

Ogaga asked, 'I wanted to know what has happened, and what needs to be done now? What is his diagnosis?'

'Hmm, when he came in, he had HONK. HONK stands for hyperosmolar non-ketotic diabetes. We also believed he was septic as a result. We treated him with IV antibiotics and his sugar levels are now down.'

'OK,' Ogaga responded. 'I looked at his drug chart and he was on blood pressure medication, amlodipine. His chart also shows he is on metformin and gliclazide for his diabetes, simvastatin to control his cholesterol, and quetiapine?' Ogaga gazed at Dr Ogunsola with a queried look and his head tilted to the side. 'What was the quetiapine for?'

'The quetiapine was for the psychotic behaviour he was displaying,' Dr Ogunsola replied.

Ogaga's eyes widened. 'Is that what you used? What psychiatric diagnosis have you made? My dad looked and sounded normal now that I just spoke to him.'

'Well, some of the nurses have reported him touching them and chasing them around the ward at night time.'

Ogaga dared not suggest perhaps that was normal for him.

'OK,' Ogaga said, 'so does he still need to stay in hospital?'

'Well,' Dr Ogunsola said, 'we've done all we can do for him. The only thing we recommend is that he has a CT scan of his brain with regards to these psychotic symptoms, and for us to see him in our outpatient clinic in two weeks.'

Ogaga thanked Dr Ogunsola for her time and for the explanation. He wasn't sure if he was unsatisfied with the care his dad had received or if he was unsatisfied with the conversation he just had with Dr Ogunsola. He left anyway.

After leaving, he met with two of his older brothers and they left together for their father's house. On the way he relayed his conversation with Dr Ogunsola to his brothers. He also handed over another wad of thousands of nairas to Kevwe to settle the hospital bills for their dad to come home. This was when he found out from Kevwe that the house wasn't ready for their dad to return home. They had to change his mattress and fit a couple of burglar-proof doors to prevent access to unwelcome guests. They also hadn't changed the lock and key for his bedroom.

Ministry of Prayer

'Every calabash that knows my Moses, be broken now in the name of Jesus,' Amen the congregation choroused. 'Every spirit that is blocking my destiny, die by fire in the name of Jesus!' And so the prayers rang out repeatedly, over and over. It was eight pm, and the fifty strong members were in full flow; some were marching up and down the aisle, others were rolling, some banging their head on the altar.

In the name of the Holy Trinity we prayed. Amen the congregation chorused. The assistant pastor was in a frenzy, huge beads of sweat had arisen on his forehead and were working their way down to the small of his back.

Lights were out, so they had the generator on. At two am the petrol in the generator had started to run out; Pastor Steve hurriedly closed the prayer meeting. 'You are blessed and highly favoured, you are above and not beneath, you are excellent and the child of a King. Go in peace, no evil shall touch your dwelling, no evil eye shall see you, for you is prosperity and life. Amen'. And the congregation chorused amen! They started to troop out. It was already dark outside and they would all have to walk home in the dark. Thankfully the moonlight was bright and many of them lived close by.

There was one woman who seemed to not have got the memo as she stayed on her knees near the altar, whispering prayers. Everyone else had now left. Pastor Steve walked up to her, and said they have all gone. She threw her headscarf from around her head onto her shoulders, she looked up at Steve, as she knew him, and smiled.

'Quick, go through the curtains. I'll be with you shortly.'

Onajevwe moved furtively and entered behind the curtains into the hallway. She turned to the left and continued till she reached the second door on her right side. The room was unlocked. She slid in and sat on the couch in the middle of the apartment.

The apartment was at the back of the church. Miracle, faith and deliverance centre at two rooms for the presiding pastors. The senior pastor lived in a house with his family. The assistant pastor, Steve, had now been posted to the Mile

Twelve branch for the last eighteen months. He had recently qualified as a clergy two years ago and this was his first posting. It wasn't a very lucrative position: the church paid him a nominal wage of thirty thousand naira monthly, but on the other hand they provided accommodation, transport and he ate many meals at the senior pastor's home.

He met Onajevwe a couple of months ago during one of their deliverance services. She self-confessed that she had a *mammiwater* spirit. Steve remained astonished at the things that people believed; he didn't believe that *mammiwater* spirits possessed people. This provided him with a source of livelihood, as he often offered private deliverance services to clients who were willing to pay, as long as they ensured they would not inform the senior pastor or any other church members.

It was in one of the deliverance services with Onajevwe, that their consummate affair began. He couldn't help himself as she was shouting and jumping up and down during their deliverance service, and her breasts were also jumping up and down with her; she wasn't young any more, but what a body.

He had in the past had his fair share of sexual escapades with members of the choirs. He usually avoided congregation members, unless they were dating; he found this prevented him from being in the limelight. Steve was forty years of age, and he had found the collar after many years of joblessness on the streets of Lagos. Since that first day with Onajevwe, he couldn't shake himself of her.

He had come to learn she had been divorced for over fifteen years and she had two grown-up children.

Steve turned the doorknob and entered the room. He then locked the door firmly behind him, even though he knew there was nobody else in the entire building; then again, he always felt someone was watching him. The ferocity of his prayers helped to wash his sins away.

He went straight to the bed. Onajevwe came and joined him. She was very understanding; she always left before dawn and always went through the back, which was heavily covered by trees and bushes, so if anyone saw her, they could never guess that she was coming from the church. Besides, on the nights she was staying over she would tell her family she was going for all-night prayers.

Chapter Seven

His older brothers Ben and Kevwe regaled him with tales of all that had happened in the preceding two weeks. Of how they turned up with the police at night time to bust Daddy out of the house. They had been there in the morning to see him after Ben had informed them of the grave concerns about Pa Otutu's health. They had faced so much drama with Modupe, thankfully they had been able to apply wisdom and let the law deal with the matter.

He recalled the times when he was being bombarded with phone calls. First when he was in London. He had received a phone call from one of his elder brothers that Dad was sick; he had apparently been locked up in his bedroom by the mistress whom Pa Otutu had brought into the house as his concubine. As a result, he wasn't taking his diabetic medications. Somehow this woman had kept everyone from seeing him. She fed him and would lock the door and go out. It took the intervention of Pa Otutu's children, who came with the police and had the woman arrested.

When they had busted open the door, they found Pa Otutu on what was supposed to be his bed. Which essentially was a thick piece of foam that lay on the ground in the dark upstairs room. It was the middle of the night when all these incidents occurred. The concubine was dragged to a police station and kept overnight on charges of grievous bodily harm.

Meanwhile, Pa Otutu was rushed in a taxi at night time from Mile Twelve to hospital. They stopped at a few hospitals along the way, as many hospitals didn't want to take him. They thought he wouldn't make it: this was a common practice in Nigerian hospitals. They were afraid of taking on patients who looked like they would die. They didn't want to be blamed by families for their relatives dying. A dreadful thought when you consider then where do these patients go?

They eventually arrived at Badagry military hospital, where they were told they didn't think they could do much for him. However, the three sons who were with him insisted the doctors did all that they could do. He was admitted by the medical officer and started on a drip; he was also given insulin as his sugar levels read as high. He was very dehydrated.

He had blood tests that showed he didn't have malaria or typhoid infection. The urine test showed the presence of a urine infection and glucose in the urine. He spent two weeks in hospital before they felt he was ready to be discharged.

The doctors and medical staff were surprised by the progress he had made. His children were relieved that he pulled through and was alive. It was apparent to them that the old man couldn't die now; there were too many unresolved issues, and there was the new complication with the court case they had just become embroiled in with one Mr Yakubu. He was claiming Dad had sold the house to him and he had paid Dad. There was no deed of sales; the deed of the house was in Pa Otutu's name and that was with Ben. The children still had to go to court anyway. This was Nigeria, and in Nigeria you don't take anything for granted.

He was still in hospital when Ogaga arrived, because there were some medical bills to be settled before they would discharge him home. Ogaga told his brothers he couldn't see Dad again before he left, as he was flying out the next day. He gave Ben some money for transport and also just because he knew Ben was expecting this.

The First Compound
In Urhobo culture marriage wasn't strictly between one man and one woman. It meant anything from a man and one woman, to a man and as many women as he could afford. As great as this sounded it didn't often work out well, especially nowadays. Many men married more than one wife when they couldn't afford to look after one wife. Others married one or two wives, then sired children with other women. Pa Otutu when he started wasn't one of these men, he could afford it.

A traditional Urhobo man could marry as many wives as he wanted, but it was frowned upon for women to have more than one male partner, and this was greatly discouraged in many cultures. There are actually very good reasons for it, other than one would suppose from the general Western dictum that this was chauvinism in one of its common forms.

The smallest unit of kinship in Urhobo culture is not the biological family of father-mother-children, but the children of one mother, known in Urhobo as *anurhoro* (gates). Urhobo families can be a matricentric family, in this sense not different from the rest of the world where many family units consist of a mother and her children, and the father could be involved or not involved. In Urhobo culture these matricentric families existed within the framework of a larger polygynous family which lived in a complex or compound.

Pa Otutu had been married several times, at the same time as far as Ogaga and his siblings could remember. He had been married to six women at most at the same time. He married his first wife at the age of eighteen. He had his first son at the age of nineteen. His first son was now late: he had died in a car accident while accompanying a funeral procession to a friend's village.

His first son wasn't the product of the union between him and his first wife. But of his second wife. The marriage to the second wife wasn't much longer after his first marriage, albeit that the mother of his first son was already pregnant at the time. It would turn out that she didn't have much longevity in the house. In Pa Otutu's family there were the wives who were stalwarts, and there were those that in a sense passed through for some seasons.

His first wife gave birth to Ben as her first son; Ben would become the oldest child in the family after the passing of the first child. Pa Otutu went on to marry four more wives, making a total of six. He had twenty-five recognised children from about seven gates. When we say recognised, we mean children that grew up in his presence or were made known to the other children and family at some point.

On one such occasion during the dry season about three decades ago, one of his ex-wives, who was divorced sixteen years prior to that year, walked into the compound and introduced his son of sixteen years. She had left sixteen years ago, leaving her daughters. At that time the younger daughter, Uvieme, was still living with Pa Otutu. This was how Oyibo was introduced to the rest of the family.

A couple of years after that incident, another of his ex-wives brought home his son who had lived with her for the past twenty-one years in Delta state. This son was Igho, and this was how Igho came to live with the rest of the family. From then he lived with Pa Otutu in the family compound, and got to know the rest of his brothers and sisters before he went off to university.

The remarkable thing about Pa Otutu's children was that they all drew a striking resemblance to him. It was unmistakable that this was his child when you were presented with them. They usually had the same forehead, eyebrows and the same deep-set facial structures, such as his prominent orbital ridges. They all shared the same broad handsome features.

Ogaga not only recalled the children of ex-wives that they found out about throughout their childhood and teenage years. He also remembered the stories his mother, Ochuko, told him of the children of his concubines. There were the reported two girls born to one Yoruba woman; Kevwe said those ones were in London. He had actually accused Ochuko of knowing where they were. This came about when he was searching for the names and locations of all Pa Otutu's children.

Since his last child, who was called Chuk, was born, he didn't have any other children. When Ogaga had been staying with his father, there were sixteen children in the house at the same time, as well as three wives. They lived in the family house, which was a massive sixteen-bedroom house, with six bathrooms and toilets, three living rooms and two kitchens. The property sat in the middle of a large compound. Ogaga remembered playing all sorts of games in this compound. It was so large they played football in the front of the compound.

They played five-aside to seven-a-side games. They

hosted their own mini Olympics, with games such as high jump, long jump, lawn tennis, wrestling, basketball and long-distance running. Obviously, the long-distance running didn't take place within the compound; it involved a race between Ogaga and his brothers around the small township in which they lived near Mile Twelve. Usually about six of the siblings would take part in this race, partly because some were too young, and others were too mature and busy working or gallivanting around the town. These were very fond memories that Ogaga treasured.

Many times, their schoolmates came round to play football with them, eat with them and play all sorts of games. On reflection, Ogaga found it incredulous that they had enough for an Otutu football team and basketball team; they could have sent an entourage to the Olympics in Ogaga's imagination. He always liked the sense of belonging that coming from a big family had brought, and the sense of power that you could be anything you wanted to be.

Ogaga remembered they grew up in a town near Mile Twelve. They had previously lived in Obanikoro, but had moved to the new house that Pa Otutu built in Mile Twelve, around 1990, just before Ogaga turned five years of age. This was how they came to live in the place Ogaga referred to as the first compound; the children belonging to each *anurhorho* (gate) had their rooms close to their mother or, in the case of the first wife who had eight children, had their section of the house.

The Court House
The day had come, with Pa Otutu in the hospital, that Mr Yakubu tried to make his advantage felt. He finally revealed

his hand. The mastermind behind the plot, he filed a suit which was served to Pa Otutu on his hospital bed. He was sueing Pa Otutu for fraud. He claimed they had agreed that he would buy the house for fifteen million naira, but after he had paid the money Pa Otutu remained in the house and refused to draw up a memorandum of sale. The summons stipulated that Pa Otutu or a representative of his was to appear before the civil courts within two weeks to answer the case.

The case was to be heard by a solitary judge and not a jury. Mr Yakubu had visited the judge the week before in his office, and after greeting him he placed some wads of nairas on the table, which he informed the judge was a gift. The male judge simply nodded his head in agreement, smiled, opened a drawer under his desk and slid in the bundle where there were a few other bundles from previous visitors that day.

After Mr Yakubu had explained how he hoped the judge would help him and what the case involved, the judge simply asked him if he had any evidence showing that the sale had been protracted to him. Or did he have any receipt that he paid him the amount of money he had stipulated? Mr Yakubu replied no to this. The judge explained that he was afraid the law would have to decide, as in this case they had to uphold the law, and in every case, they must always appear to uphold the law, or else what would become of the country?

It seemed the judge wasn't swayed by the gift; it wasn't an unusual practice in Nigeria. And as far as the judge was concerned, he hadn't accepted a bribe nor would he be accepting one.

As Mr Yakubu got up, the judge didn't hand back to him his wads of naira, after all it was a gift. He simply smiled and nodded him to the door, as the prosecutor for another of his cases walked in.

Ben attended court on behalf of Pa Otutu, with the family lawyer. The presiding judge heard both sides of the argument. He had reviewed the case the night before, examining all the evidence and arguments that were put before him. He made sure to apply the law as best as he saw fit. In every possible case he always upheld the law. After deliberating for about thirty minutes, he decided Mr Yakubu hadn't provided enough evidence to support his claim: there was no evidence to suggest he had any claim to the house.

He ruled that Mr Otutu should pay the sum of fifteen million naira, which he deemed to be owed to Mr Yakubu; however, Mr Yakubu had no claim to the house, as it wasn't plausible that a house of that size should sell for fifteen million, and there was no documentation to support it. He ruled that the money owed should be pursued through mediation between both parties and not the courts. He also split the cost of the court between both parties.

The ruling was fair. However, this left Mr Yakubu in a conundrum, how did he obtain fifteen million naira from Mr Otutu on his sick bed? It looked as if that if his illness was unto death, Pa Otutu would win this game of chess.

Down Sapele Road

Kawere gang were having a party tonight: they had a new recruit. Brohen had been kidnapped earlier today from the Sapele area. One of the gang members had found him walking along a bushy path on a side road. He had quickly pulled by, snatched him up and put him in the back of the car and drove to the den.

Once it was day, Brohen was let out. Brohen cried incessantly, '*Oni me, Ose me,* (my mother, my father).' In reply he received a dirty slap from the boss of the gang, Captain. Captain had been leading the Kawere gang for the last five years.

They started off initially with plundering oil pipes and selling oil illegally. Then they found even more lucrative than this was the kidnap and request for ransom for white foreigners who worked for the oil companies. This naturally led to the kidnap of all white foreigners.

It was only two months ago that they had made it big again. In this business one payoff was never enough; there were too many mouths to feed in order to be successful.

'Brohen! Come here.'

'Yes, Sir.'

'How old are you?'

'I am eleven years old.'

'Do you know why you are here?'

Brohen shook in his raggedy brown shorts and holey shirt, '*Mi gwono mli oni me.*' (I want to see my mother,)

Thwaa! Another heavy slap followed, with Brohen falling to the floor.

'Do you know why you are here?' Captain repeated.

Brohen whimpered, 'I don't know.'

'Pick yourself from the floor, you now work for me. Don't worry, I'll look after you. Ehm Bender, give him this.' Captain handed Bender, another of his henchmen, a lit spliff to give to Brohen to smoke.

Brohen smoked it for about two seconds before he broke into coughing bouts… and the surrounding entourage erupted in laughter.

Captain got up from his seat, waved his hand at those standing by, and left. They would return tonight, they had a party every night a new recruit was brought in.

Chapter Eight

Sixteen months ago

It was the tenth day of the month. Ben had been living on edge for the past few weeks. Now he was back in a different hospital, with Pa Otutu taken ill again after collapsing at home. In the last two weeks Pa Otutu had become more unwell. In fact, a week ago he had felt faint and collapsed. Ben had to press on his chest to get him to wake up. A few days before this they had been arguing as usual. When this episode happened, Ben swore never to have another argument with his dad.

It was only two weeks ago that Pa Otutu and Ben went for a walk around Agility. Many of his neighbours, friends and acquaintances were surprised and, in some cases, glad to see him. After the way he had been rushed to hospital and the reports that they had been hearing, they weren't sure they would see him alive again.

Ese was also around. It didn't seem as if Pa Otutu was responding to treatment this time. Kevwe walked in and then Pa Otutu started to talk. He thanked them for their care, and he charged Kevwe with completing the house he started building again in Kokori. 'Remember I've already bought all the furniture, including a fridge and a freezer; they are in Uncle Jo's house.'

Pa Otutu had been making great preparations to go back to live in Kokori before he took ill. He had immediately reconnected with his cousins and his nephews, many of whom he had paid for their schooling fees when they were growing up. He asked Ben to speak to Uncle Amos with regards to getting the furniture back to the house in preparation for him. He had been preparing for this homecoming now for over two years.

Onajevwe and Irhorho had gone up to prepare some food for Pa Otutu, and they would be back later that evening. Later that evening, Ben, Ese, Kevwe, Onajevwe, Irhorho and Efe were around Pa Otutu's bedside just keeping him company; well, the girls were mostly fussing over him. It was a strange feeling that they felt, the man that they were so close to but yet so distant from, the man they loved but also feared in some form of ridiculous way. As for Onajevwe, this was the man that didn't turn up to her wedding because her husband wasn't Urhobo or even from Delta state. Her ex-husband was of the Tive tribe. Pa Otutu had thrown her out of the house, but when her marriage failed, he had welcomed her and his grandchildren into his home.

It was a lovely evening for all; they sat and stood around his bedside until the moonlight was full in the sky. The crickets could be heard chirping through the ward's windows, which were bereft of mosquito nets. Occasionally, a toad could also be heard croaking. After the children had both tired themselves and tired Pa Otutu out, they all left, feeling content in their heart, yet with a certain heaviness. It had been a trip down memory lane. It had also been a moment for them to sit proverbially at their father's feet. As he uttered both wise words and at times gibberish that old men tend to say. Well, the children felt that way when a saying came forth and the children were unsure of why and where the statement was going.

The next day the children came and went as usual. At times Pa Otutu was clear in his thoughts, but these periods grew shorter and shorter, as he seemed to be sleeping most of the time. On the third day when Ben and Ese arrived at eight am in the morning, they walked to Pa Otutu's side, and as they said Daddy *Miguo*, there was no answer.

They walked up to him and shook him, there was no response. They turned him from his side to his front, and there was Pa Otutu, frozen, expressionless, and he was starting to feel cold to touch. Ese and Ben chorused loudly for a nurse or doctor to come quickly. Then all commotion broke loose.

Broken Calabash

Pastor Steven couldn't believe the betrayal; on an off chance the senior pastor had discovered the relationship between him and Onajevwe. He had come knocking one Sunday evening, and discovered Pastor Steven between Onajevwe's legs.

'So it is true,' screamed the senior pastor. 'I didn't want to believe it, but really "the bird doesn't settle by chance". I wanted to believe it were merely a rumour… (his words stuck in his throat).'

'Sir, please, it is the work of the enemy, it won't happen again.'

'Common shut up, it has been happening all this while, what do you mean it won't happen again?'

Onajevwe had scurried under the covers. Pastor Steven

had started to remonstrate with the senior pastor and had forgotten to bring his trousers up from his ankles.

'Would you get dressed, leave and never come back. If it were not for the disgrace it would bring to the church, I would have announced it at our next meeting. I will tell the congregation you have been urgently assigned due to unforeseen circumstances.' He gestured wildly at the two of them. 'I don't want to see you two here again, children of apostasy,' he snarled, kissing his teeth as he turned around.

As chance would have it, Onajevwe had lost her father two weeks ago. She invited him to come and live with her, and they moved into her father's previous bedroom. He guessed their deliverance would continue. It was no longer her deliverance. He had chosen the collar as the churches were the epitome of structure in a chaotic Nigeria. They paid on time and without fail. He now had no source of livelihood, but at least he had a roof over his head. He was basically now stuck with Onajevwe, for without her he might as well move under a bridge.

She had suggested to him to open his own church: a very good idea he thought. 'Deliverance and restoration ministry'. The name had a ring to it.

As for Onajevwe, her husband left her many years ago, and her father had died. She needed somebody, she almost couldn't stand the pity with which people looked at her any more.

Chapter Nine

The day

'*The night has gone; the morning has come. It appears the chickens have come home to roost.*'

What a raucous gathering; the commotion was unbelievable. The onlookers looked on from under their canopies, and the families beheld from their shelter in the house, and there were those that stood by the gate, as they attempted to reason with the mob. There were all sorts of people: young men in work trousers and polo shirts with their hard-worn looks; old women with scarves and equally old wrappers with their earth-worn faces. There were also many boisterous young men, with ripped muscles evident as they were topless; they had obviously worked out most days of their life under the Kokori sun. With plenty shouting, smacking and running to and fro, the components of this commotion were established.

The ambulance had finally arrived; they had to wait for it, fight for it, now it looked as if the real fight had just begun. It was nearly four o' clock; they started setting up the rest of the canopies at eleven am—the earliest arrivals had been around twelve pm. It looked like the planning and actioning of this process started today and by some miracle they hoped it would finish today. As the nose of the ambulance entered the front of the compound, its siren had only been heard a few minutes earlier: the people had waited all day for the coffin to arrive.

Many onlookers were milling in the street, some street hawkers had set up shop at the front of the compound. There were numerous vehicles parked on the streets. Some were taxis looking for business, some were the vehicles of various vendors and some were the vehicles that had brought members of the party to the occasion.

It was a relief; the fear was that it might never come. If only some knew that there might never have been a coffin; there might never had been an ambulance; the body could have been left in the mortuary, which had been its home for the last fifteen months. When it made the long journey from Lagos state to Kokori in Delta state, it was a choice of logistics and cost. It had been determined that the funeral would be held in Kokori Delta state. Moreover, the cost of the body's stay in Lagos was three hundred naira a week, but in Kokori it would be one hundred naira a week. A straightforward logistical decision.

Getting the body from Lagos to Kokori had required a phone call from Lagos to London in order to solicit money to hire the vehicle and to pay for the hotel fees for three men who seemed to be the men in charge of the matter at hand. They were in charge and had the ability to recall resources from London? One of their younger siblings had sent money from the money exchange in Peckham. The transfer rate was four hundred and fifty naira to one pound; it was still, however, a lot of money, more than the average monthly mortgage in London.

There was no sign of the promised security, for which eighty thousand naira had been allocated. No army-clad uniformed Nigerian soldiers running around, standing to attention or even hiding somewhere, anywhere. No vigilante group or black-clad Nigerian police officers who stayed reasonably happy as long as you gave them several bottles of schnapps. This was also part of the budget. Well, it appears this event was going to pot, just as the budget, which had been sent fifteen months ago, went up in smoke. The children in London had argued with the senior children in Nigeria that the budget seemed excessive. They had given all sorts of reasons: saying things are expensive, and it is the elders. 'They are very wicked. They are taxing us. You should have been there at our first meeting. They wanted to strip Ben and beat him. We had to explain the circumstances of the death to them.'

The position of the elders in Urhobo culture meant one of their roles was to ensure a man's children got what was rightfully theirs when a man died, but as well that the children bore the responsibility and liabilities of the deceased. It was no surprise that the elders tended to focus on imposing the 'said liabilities', and as they saw necessary. Slipping in some extra liabilities as they saw fit.

As the ambulance edged into the compound, it could proceed no further for it was immediately surrounded by a swarm of people. The mob had jumped on the bonnet of the ambulance, demanding it would not enter the compound until their demands were met. The more the driver of the ambulance honked, the more the mob pressed against the bonnet of the ambulance, smashing the palms of their hands into the hood, shouting, *'We no go gree, this ambulance no go pass (*we will not let this ambulance pass).'

Onlookers derided the family of the man who had brought this occasion about. Many said, '*Shuo, I never see matter like this* (we've never seen anything like this).'

Shuo is a remark that is used to express a disturbing or disgusting surprise one feels towards an event.

There were mainly middle-aged and elderly ladies in traditional attire, shaking their heads vigorously in a fashion that could not be described as gentle. A few of the visitors who had been present from earlier on in the day began to think the worst of what the day would bring. They certainly thought in their minds, 'what a disgrace, what shenanigans is this?' In so many ways the truth about Nigeria is that there are so many unnecessary dramas, and there often was drama at all events; from naming ceremonies, birthday celebrations, funerals and definitely marriages.

There are always event profiteers; it seems marriages and burials are the places where families distribute a portion of their wealth to strangers, albeit unwillingly. To be a bit more accurate, where strangers who at will morphed into a distant or close relative seek the wealth that truly belongs to them, or that their status deserved.

Thank goodness it wasn't raining; for if it had been, the day would have been dreadful. This was not a calamity of errors; the children would refer to this as wickedness. Pa Otutu's children who came from London felt that the older ones ought to examine themselves. After several trips to the money exchange shop in Peckham and the transfer of several thousands of pounds in the last sixteen months, running to a bill of more than eight thousand pounds. Not taking into account the other finances that had come from the United States and Australia with individuals visiting respective

Western Unions or an equivalent money exchange of sorts.

The squabble was over money; the mob consisted of some that claimed that one of the man's sons, who was commissioned to refurbish the house, owed them money for materials used in building the house, and he hadn't paid them. The sum of the money totalled three hundred thousand naira. This was not the first such claim or threat to the proceedings of the day. There were other parties claiming lesser ridiculous sums: one young man was owed sixty thousand naira for putting up two doors; another was owed thirty thousand naira for plastering the grave site. It was ridiculous. At the rate of hire these parties were claiming, one would be a millionaire if they put up twenty doors or if they plastered forty grave sites; life would be easy.

There were some who never thought that this day would come. The summation of this homecoming some would say started some sixteen months ago; others would say it started sixty-eight years ago. It all depends from which perspective you were looking from. Some of the man's children had not even bothered to come for the day. They had relayed their messages across the oceans to the rest of the family. They contributed four hundred thousand naira to the burial cause and, as it appeared that very little headway had been made, they said, 'What has it got to do with us? As far as we are concerned, we have contributed what we feel is significant and enough to bury the old man.'

Two out of three of this group of children who were born to one mother lived in USA and Australia respectively. They had cut themselves off from this process, perhaps with the thought that the old man would never be buried. Even their immediate younger brother who lived in Lagos had been so vocal about the whole process during the preparations, but when it came to it, he didn't even make the journey to Kokori.

How could one live with the knowledge that after their father had died, he might not be buried? And the person was very much alive, so how truly could it have nothing to do with you? Surely, we will all die one day.

Industrialisation and commercialisation have changed the nature of Urhobo burials. Families frequently refrigerate their deceased relatives for months. This allows indigenous Urhobo people who have died overseas, or somewhere other than Urhoboland in Nigeria, to be transported back to Urhoboland. Importantly, it allows for a corpse to be refrigerated until the family of the deceased can gather money, then convene to celebrate the life of their loved one.

In the case of certain individual children, 'loved one' might not necessarily apply, judging from their actions.

Chapter Ten

The first compound

The compound in Mile Twelve was the first place that Ogaga recognised as the compound. From the time that they moved there, it was here that Ogaga started to be able to understand. It was here that he attended most of his primary education. Pa Otutu's younger children basically started that school. It started with the immediate Ruemu who was one of the first three students of the school. He was followed by Ogaga, Choja and Kokori who were the next set in the school. The school grew from this point.

The school gained attention when Ruemu gained a scholarship by becoming the number one student in the whole of Lagos state on the common entrance exam. Pa Otutu rejected the offer of the scholarship outright, citing that 'he was well able to look after his children and educate them fully'. Time will tell that he only educated his eldest daughter fully until she finished university. With the rest of his children, after he had educated them to secondary school level, their education was either taken over by their mothers, or by the child themselves, or they never completed their education as of this day.

Such was the pride of Pa Otutu. He always commanded his children, 'do not eat outside', 'do not take things from strangers', and at times he would even forbid some children from going to a certain person's house. Much of this was because of his fears and his desire to protect them. He would give this advice which he felt would keep his children and family safe. Sometimes it was more than safety, it was about his pride; his statement to the world that he has many children and he can very well provide for them.

In Agility things had started to change. Pa Otutu was a very rich man; he had made a lot of money and he owned businesses, some of which had now collapsed. He had a poultry farm in Kokori, he had previously had a motor company, and he had built numerous houses with varying outcomes. The government had seized one of his properties, another sank into the ground, and now the last house standing was the house in Agility. The compound where the younger set of his children would grow up.

Pa Otutu was a man who thought big, but it appears he didn't have the discipline to keep in the wealthy bracket. He had come from nothing in his little Kokori village, learning herbs and the way of healing from his mother. He built up a few companies. In the olden days whenever he travelled to Kokori on the mission of looking after the farm, he had often been found in bed with a concubine rather than running the farm. Consequently, the poultry died and all on the farm was lost. The same could be told of the car company where his enthusiasm and thinking got things started; he simply never demonstrated the discipline that these sorts of projects required to maintain their success.

Pa Otutu got his first break when he healed his headmaster

in school. Yes, it is true he was also called 'doctor Otutu'; even though he never went to a school of medicine. His headmaster was unwell in secondary school and, using his knowledge of herbs that he gained from his mum, he was able to cure him. This led to him receiving a free secondary education at the school. His next big break came with his first big job.

He healed the manager of the Central Bank of Nigeria, which was one of the biggest banks in Nigeria at the time. This led to him being employed by the Central Bank of Nigeria, and earning a substantial salary in return. He married his first wife at the age of eighteen, he had his first son at the age of nineteen years, married five more wives and had many more children afterwards. His genealogy read like a biblical story.

Knowing of his achievements, especially in the area of healing, you had to respect Dr Otutu. There are many quacks and traditional healers, who engage in various rituals, promising healing and wholeness to the unfortunate persons who turned to them from desperation. There are true stories. One of a man who was sick following a stroke in the hospital. He made a reasonable enough recovery so that he was able to transfer, but not able to walk.

After several weeks his family could no longer afford his medical bills, so they discharged him and took him to a herbalist. The herbalist set a fire in his little hut and began the ritual. As the herbalist danced around the fire, the man with the stroke slipped from his chair and fell into the—now roaring—fire. His mobility was limited so he couldn't get out of the fire, and it took a few minutes before the bystanders got him out of the fire.

He had sustained twenty-five percent burns by then. His relatives rushed him back to the hospital with third degree burns covering the half of his body that had been paralysed by the stroke. This unfortunate soul ended up in a worse state than when he started.

As for Pa Otutu, his prowess with herbs was legendary. People came from far and wide to seek his help. He had been known to cure people of mental ailments, eczema and snake bites. He had a legendary concoction which he called *Ifue*. He used this for snake bites, scorpion bites and wound infections depending on what he decided to throw into the mix of this concoction.

There was a point when all the younger sets of children had eczema. Pa Otutu made a concoction of palm oil and salt, and rubbed it all over them for a few days. Their eczema cleared within a week.

Many were dubious, but what was clear was that his methods were effective This was evidenced by the favourable situations that came to him as a result of his gift, and the large cash gifts he received after he had been in pain, either when one of his clients or a relative of a previous client decided to visit to extend their gratitude many days after the cured illness.

Ogaga remembered once when a client of Pa Otutu's client brought a patient for him. She was an eighteen-year-old girl who had a mental illness. She stayed in the family house in a room by herself. She would often strip, run around the compound naked, and even stabbed one of Ogaga's older brothers, Kokori, with a fork on his head.

Within a few weeks she was cured. Pa Otutu often used a combination of herbal mixtures and animal sacrifices. Sometimes he made herbs for them to bath in. The sacrifices represented where he came from. He was a traditionalist that also dealt in rituals and occultic practices for the purposes of healing. Like many Urhobos of his generation he believed in the realm of the ancestors. That is prayers could be offered to one's ancestors in order to get favours from them.

There was myriad of notable experiences that happened in Pa Otutu's compound. The house was so arranged that the three wives that lived with him had their rooms, the oldest children had their rooms, and the younger children shared rooms according to their age group and sex and sometimes according to who their mother was.

The youngest girls tended to stay with their mothers, and the boys who belonged to a particular mother tended to stay together in one room. The rest of the house was shared. The five toilets, four bathrooms and the massive living and dining space at the front of the house in which during Ogaga's early years sat a large lovely marble table with yellow and brownish weaving patterns decorating it.

Ruemu had chipped his tooth on this table during play with his other siblings. The table itself was eventually broken in half during play; by whom Ogaga couldn't really remember. But he remembered that they were playing. Family legend has it that it was Ruemu's head that snapped the table in half: Ruemu had a big head.

Walking from the living room there was a long corridor that stretched right to the back of the house. At the back of the house there was a spiral staircase that led upstairs, and directly in front there were three rooms all lined up in a row. The first room to the left-hand side was called 'last room', christened and accepted by all the children as it was the last room at the back of the house. The middle room was called 'blue room', as it was blue in colour, and the room on the right was called 'yellow room', as the walls were coloured yellow.

In the space intervening from the living room to the rooms at the back of the house there were two kitchens on the left-hand side, a toilet and three other rooms on the right-hand side. After going up the concrete stairs there were mostly rooms. A row of four rooms were on each side of the corridor, which led to another large living space that was specifically for Pa Otutu; his bedroom was through the living space and it was en-suite. To the left and anterior to the living space there was a large veranda with an open mouth that overlooked the front of the compound and 'Bisi Adelesi Street' where they lived.

From here Pa Otutu could sit down with whatever he fancied, perhaps a jug of palm wine and keep an eye on his household, seeing all that was happening in the compound below him where the children played, and watching the happenings up and down Bisi Adelesi Street. One could see all the way to the top of the street, where Bisi Adelesi Street met the junction, and one could see as far as the yellow house to the right, where one of the children's neighbours lived. Segun and Ojo often came to Otutu's compound to play with Pa Otutu's children and also to eat with them.

There was a spot in the parlour downstairs where Pa Otutu would sit down from time to time and at times gather all his children or whoever he could find. Sitting on a lower stool would be his favourite son, Ruemu. He would put his hat (much like a cowboy hat) on his head and teach Ruemu to pour out drink libations to the forefathers. He would call out *'Idhararhe nnowe, usifu nnowe'*. That is to mean 'Hear me Idhararhe, Usifu'; these were the names of his father, his father's father and his grandfather's father. He sometimes would go up until the fourth generation.

Then he would offer his prayers, pouring out a small

portion of vodka onto the ground with each prayer uttered. This was a common practice among the Urhobos. They believed their forefathers are with them even after death. To Ogaga it seemed more of the concept of 'the living dead'. The Urhobos believed dead loved ones are not gone forever and live in the spirit realm. There are obviously some slight variations to this belief. They believe God *Oghene* lives in heaven *Odjuvwu*, while *Erivwin*, the place where the dead live, is under the earth. They believe the souls *Erhi* go to *Erivwin* to stay, where also dwell nature spirits *Edjoverivwi* and the divinities. Both animal and human spirits are believed to have souls *Irhi*, and once they die, they go to *Erivwin* to stay. The length of time they might remain here is debatable.

Many Urhobos believe that the spirit world is real and that one's 'living dead' interacted in this realm. They can see us, but we are prevented from seeing them by a sort of spiritual film. Pa Otutu was no exception, as he proclaimed himself a Christian; however, many Urhobo men and women still held ancestral beliefs and believed they could be protected from harm by their fathers and also given blessings when they invoked their names.

For many years there was a stain at the particular spot where the drink offerings were poured out. The spot where Ruemu, on many occasions, wore his dad's hat and held his feathered fan to be the oracle in his father's house. Ogaga wasn't sure oracle was the right word to use, as he never brought back any message from the living dead, perhaps more a mediator or sort of priest who delivered prayers and libations that he was too young to understand.

Chapter Eleven

The Journey Home

Ochuko had gone ahead of her children to make the necessary preparations for the funeral. Ogaga arrived three days before the event; his brother Ruemu arrived on the evening flight. They had planned to catch an early flight from Lagos to Warri.

On the plane from London Heathrow to Lagos, Ogaga's heart was full of trepidation; this was so unusual for him. He normally had an inner calm that was seldom troubled, regardless of what life threw at him.

Ogaga sat next to his wife on the flight. His belly flopped and turned with every jolt of turbulence that the aircraft experienced. It would be OK his wife whispered in his right ear; having seen the look on his face. Since he had started packing for the flight to Nigeria, Ogaga's mind was full of thoughts of death; morbid thoughts of his own mortality and of his dad's mortality flooded his mind. It was as though somehow his mortality had strangely become linked to the demise of his father, even though this was over a year ago; to be more precise sixteen going on seventeen months ago.

Ogaga prayed continually in his heart that the flight would arrive safely, that they would make it to the village in Delta state. He prayed that the burial would hold, that there would actually be a burial place ready with canopies. As far as they knew, they only received the date of the burial on the Whatsapp image Kevwe had sent in the 'burial group' a few weeks ago. It stated the date, but no venue, no starting time, no end time.

As soon as they had the date, Ogaga and Ruemu immediately booked their flight tickets to Nigeria. Ruemu kept going on about how this was a disgrace that it had taken this long. He had repeatedly championed throwing as much money at the problem as possible. He had given beyond what was budgeted to him; had continued to encourage Ogaga and Choja to do the same, all he cared was that the burial should hold.

'Babes, do you remember that MoneyGram incident?' Ogaga said as he tried to lighten the mood.

'Oh! Yes, when you were trying to sell my dad's old sofa on Gumtree.'

'Well, I was surprised when he didn't try to negotiate but offered to pay the full price, even though I should say I did put it up for a fair price. After all, your dad wanted to sell it for eight hundred pounds.'

Ogaga's wife burst into a giggle.

'Why are you laughing? Ogaga asked.

'Didn't you realise something was wrong? First, he said he would buy at the price, then he asked for a favour. So apparently, he was on a ship in Qatar and wasn't going to be home for a few months. He asked you to pay a shipping company through MoneyGram so that they would come and collect the sofa.'

Ogaga also giggled in his seat. 'Then me like a *mugu* gave him my Paypal email address for him to transfer the full payment including the shipping cost to me, while I went to send the four hundred pounds shipping cost.' Ogaga's giggle turned into a bit of louder laughter. 'Can you imagine!'

'Well,' Ogaga's wife said. 'God saved you. Thank God MoneyGram had blocked that account already, so the money you sent didn't go through, then he had the cheek to change the account details.'

'Hmmm!' Ogaga responded. 'It was only when the second account details appeared to be a Nigerian account did alarm bells truly start ringing; the first account was in Dubai, so the bells didn't ring too loudly. When I kept checking my Paypal account and didn't see any money, I became scared.'

Ogaga's wife chirped in, 'Well, that is why it is good you listen to me. If I hadn't told you to cancel it after you told me about it you would have lost four hundred pounds.'

'These people that do four-one-nine are getting smarter. Can you believe from the confirmation of payments he was sending me by email, it looked exactly as Paypal does when you've received a payment. It was only when I tried to click on the page that I realised none of the links on the page worked. That escape made me think how many people do they scam on a daily basis?'

'Well,' his wife responded. 'Now you know. If anything is not official and straightforward don't get involved.'

'But they are hijacking authentic companies like Gumtree and ebay,' Ogaga said in response.

Ogaga's wife started to say, 'There is this one sad story about a friend of a friend of mine. When he first came to London from Nigeria, he got a job at a construction site in Chelsea. His work name was Richard. He lived with this woman who helped him come to London, but because then he didn't have papers his pay used to go into this woman's account. He was using the same last name as the woman, whose name was Rachel Ogunleye. He was bearing Richard Ogunleye so the payroll wouldn't notice as the initials were the same.

'I'm telling you this man suffered; from his wages she used to give him just five pounds to buy Lebara top-up to call his family in Nigeria, and then money to buy an Oyster.'

The plane landed without incident at Murtala Muhammed International airport, where he and his wife disembarked around about six pm Nigerian time. It had been arranged that his cousin Uvie would pick them up, so he expected to see him outside the airport. After passing through customs, Ogaga and his wife walked to baggage reclaim to pick up their luggage. They joined the swarm of people who had gathered along the baggage carousel. All he and his wife could feel was being pressed on every side as people squeezed into every available space to get as close to the baggage carousel as possible. Surprisingly to Ogaga, it wasn't very humid.

His thoughts would change very quickly as would everybody else. As they pressed towards the large baggage carousel, some of its plates were missing, some were broken in half; this left the picture of a large carousel that appeared to have missing black teeth or half-chipped teeth, through which one hoped their luggage wouldn't fall into. Suddenly, as Ogaga pondered the makeup of this carousel, the lights went out!

Up NEPA everyone screamed in unison, as many Nigerians had come to know over the years the problems Nigeria had with maintaining electricity. The baggage carousel had also come to a complete halt, and as the mass of people at the carousel and in the airport stood in darkness, people started to switch on the torches on their smartphones. Not that this provided any meaningful light in that big auditorium. They appeared more like distant stars, as one would gaze upon the sky on a dark starry night. After about three minutes, the motor of the generator could be heard whirling and the light came back on. It took a few more minutes before the baggage carousel started moving again.

Nigeria and electricity had a fractured relationship. Nigeria somehow supplies electricity to Ghana where electricity is more constant than in Nigeria. There have been projects to build power plants for the last thirty years, and nothing has materialised. Most Nigerians know the reason why there is never constant electricity in Nigeria is because there are short-sighted people who have become stakeholders in the generator business and so make it their duty that the country will always need noisy fuel-consuming pollutant generators. Not to mention the leaders of the country who do nothing to help the average man in living his daily life.

In the meantime, baggage handlers could be seen crawling out from the hole through which the luggage was fed into, manually pushing and pulling people's luggage on the baggage carousel. Their luggage eventually arrived, they picked up their bags, refused a trolley from one of the baggage handlers, but also made sure to refuse their assistance. Ogaga opined that the baggage handlers offered their assistance not out of a sense of duty or care, but because they were hoping to solicit some money from you, by the time they assisted you to whatever vehicle was taking you from the airport.

They came outside to the usual throng of locals and taxi drivers soliciting for service. '*Oga*, do you want taxi?' a local called out.

Another called out, '*Oga*, do you want to make a phone call?' Hands grabbed at Ogaga and his wife's luggage. 'Make I help you?' they chorused.

'No thank you,' Ogaga's wife said.

Ogaga went straight into colloquial Nigerian English, '*Abeg, leave am, we dey ok.*' *Oga* is a Yoruba word meaning boss, master or sir that is used universally in the south of Nigeria as far as Ogaga was aware.

He spotted Uvie at the end of the queue of people that had come to pick up their friends and relatives; Uvie waved to him and walked towards him. Ogaga waved back and beckoned to his wife, pointing, 'There's my cousin Uvie, let's go.' As always, the first thing that could be noticed with Uvie was his stomach, regardless of whatever he was wearing, it bulged forward like the belly of a heavily pregnant woman.

Uvie embraced Ogaga and his wife. 'My sister, so good to finally meet you. I've seen your pictures from the wedding in the family group,' Uvie said. The group embraced, then Uvie grabbed a couple of their pieces of luggage and started to make his way away from the entrance. 'Follow me,' he bellowed, turning his head to his two new guests, as he bullied his way through the crowd.

'We are going to catch the bus,' he said without looking back. A frown came over Ogaga's face; he thought he would have arrived with a vehicle as per normal. Uvie continued, 'They don't let people pull up or park in front of the airport any more. You have to catch a bus to the car park.'

A young man sidled up to them and said, 'Do you want taxi?'

Ogaga said no, but Uvie asked how much. To which the

young man replied four thousand naira. Uvie kissed his teeth and kept walking. The young man, dressed in skinny dirty blue jeans and a worn yellow shirt, sidled up to him and said how much do you want?

Uvie said, 'Three thousand naira, we are going to Igando.'

'Ah! Igando is too far,' the young man said. 'Three thousand five hundred naira?'

'OK,' Uvie said. 'Where is your car?'

'In the car park,' the young man retorted. Ogaga looked confused, and then it dawned on him that Uvie didn't own a car. He felt slightly embarrassed. The young man grabbed a bag from Ogaga's wife and said, 'Let me carry that.' The crowd started to thicken as they got to the bus stop.

The bus arrived, and as its doors started to open people rushed in. 'Shine your eyes,' Uvie shouted without looking back. He threw one suitcase onto the bus, picked up a second suitcase and jumped on the bus with it. Ogaga's wife followed suit and jumped on the bus. Ogaga struggled as there were people pushing in front of him, but he managed to squeeze onto the bus as well. The young man was also on the bus with the suitcase he was carrying. They then heard a high-pitched shriek, aaaaaah!

They looked and there was a small woman falling as she entered the bus. Clutching hopelessly at air as she tumbled forward, her palms scraping Ogaga's luggage as she fell onto the floor. She turned mid-flight and started accusing the man behind her. 'You pushed me.' Then there was a thud as her back hit the floor. Ogaga wasn't sure if he imagined it or if there was a small kick out from her or was it just the flailing of her leg? 'You pushed me,' she alleged again in the midst of her sobs. Nobody paid her any attention. People rather sniggered and said how can you be falling? You see the way everybody is pushing and you are not looking after yourself.

The bus ride to the car park was cramped, with heads buried in people's sweaty armpits. There wasn't much light outside as Ogaga's wife hugged into him and they both laughed at the incredulity of the situation before them. The rest of the bus ride was uneventful and they pulled into the parking lot fifteen minutes later.

After disembarking from the bus, they followed the young man with the skinny jeans and worn yellow shirt till they got to his car. As they were loading their bags in the car, a rather large young man approached Uvie.

'Brother, I've got some free CDs I'm giving away. Would you like one?'

'No thank you,' Uvie replied.

The young man then turned to Ogaga, 'Would you like one?'

'No thanks,' Ogaga said.

'It is OK. It is gospel music,' the rather large young man said. 'I'm promoting myself, you don't need to pay anything.'

Ogaga's wife called to him and said, 'Hurry up and get in the car, I don't know what this person wants.' They got in the car and the young man in the skinny jeans and worn yellow shirt drove away from the airport and up to Igando. Ogaga thought about stories he had heard as a child of children that had accepted gifts from strangers and had been turned into either an animal such as a tortoise, or an inanimate object such as a coin, and then taken for sacrifice.

The rather large young man watched them with some hope in his eyes as they drove away. Who would actually take anything from him? In Nigeria of all places; to be taking things from large young men at just after six-thirty in the morning, when the sun hasn't even risen yet. Fraudulently soliciting money for something that was meant to be free would be the least of your worries. You could be turned into a chicken or a tortoise; that seems to be a popular one.

Home My Home

The following morning Ogaga called Ruemu back in London, informing him they had arrived. Later on that evening, Ruemu had boarded his flight and had landed safely; his friend, with whom he would be staying with at Festac, picked him up. The second morning after Ogaga and his wife arrived, they were due to be catching the eight am flight to Warri in Delta state. Warri was the commercial capital of Delta state, although Asaba was the official capital of Delta state. In the same way Lagos was the commercial capital of Nigeria, although Abuja was the official capital of Nigeria. Asaba happened to be the capital of Delta state only because a wife of one of the late presidents was from Asaba, and it was made the capital by her husband. This represents just a tinge of the nepotism that goes on in Nigeria.

Ogaga had booked the internal flights, and he had also booked for Ruemu to fly with them. Ogaga, his wife and Uvie set off at five forty am to the local airport in Lagos. They were driven by a driver by the name of Stanley. On his way he called Ruemu. 'Are you on your way to the airport?'

Ruemu replied, 'We are not leaving yet.' It sounded like Ogaga's phone call had just woken Ruemu up.

'You know the flight is at eight, and the latest you can get there is seven forty-five,' Ogaga said.

Ruemu responded. 'Gregg said it is fifteen minutes away;

we will leave at seven fifteen.'

'Well, just as long as you don't miss the flight,' Ogaga said. He had one of his feelings again: that Ruemu hadn't made any plans at all, and hadn't heeded his warnings that he should wake up and leave early. He hoped he wouldn't miss the flight.

As it happened, Ruemu missed the flight; it turned out Festac was not fifteen minutes away from the airport, and apparently there was some traffic. Ruemu had to book another flight; however, there remained no more flights to Warri that day. The day was Friday; the burial was tomorrow on Saturday. Uvie had remained at the airport waiting for Ruemu to arrive. Ruemu arrived at five minutes to eight, but they didn't let him check in. Festac is apparently forty-five minutes from the local airport in Lagos in the absence of traffic. Well, Ruemu knew that now.

There was a flight to Benin which was a city about an hour and a half away from Delta state. Ruemu paid the fare to Benin; the flight didn't leave till ten am.

Ogaga and his wife arrived at Warri at nine am. A family friend Onyekan picked them up and drove them to Okpara inland which was their mum's village. He dropped them at their mum's sister's house where they would be staying for the majority of their time in Delta state.

Okpara and Kokori lay next to each other; it is a twenty-minute drive from Okpara to Kokori, which is the village Ogaga's dad came from in Urhoboland. They are part of the villages that make up the region of Agbon. The Urhobos make up the majority of Delta state, but there are other related tribes such as the Itshekiris. Also, in Delta state are the Delta Igbos. Classified as such as they are Igbo-speaking people on the same side of the river Niger as the other Delta tribes. Once you cross the river Niger you cross into Igboland starting with Anambra state.

Historically, Okpara and Kokori are siblings, that is why they have always supported each other against neighbouring villages during war times. Ogaga remembers the stories that were told to him by his mother, Ochuko, of the three founding fathers of Okpara, and how one of those three was her great-great-grandfather.

When Ogaga and his wife arrived at the house in Okpara, his mum was reported to be at her father's compound in a meeting with her younger brother Okpese. Ogaga and his wife unloaded their luggage into the house; they were very hungry at this point, but they ended up crashing on their aunt's sofas.

The Driver

After waiting several hours, Ogaga and his wife began to feel concerned about Ruemu. He had called them at about eleven thirty am and said he had landed safely and would be getting a taxi to meet them in Okpara. At two pm Ogaga called Ruemu; he said he was just entering Delta state close to Warri, and he was picking up a friend who would be directing the taxi driver to Okpara.

It was now three-thirty pm and he still wasn't there. Ogaga called him several times and couldn't get through to him. He called his friend Gregg who hadn't heard from him either. Finally, at about four pm a car was heard pulling out in front, and beeping. Ogaga rushed to the gate, went outside and saw a seven-seater Sienna vehicle, cream and black in colour. The left-hand door slid open and out stepped Ruemu.

Ogaga was relieved to see him; however, the relief was quickly replaced with a bit of frustration. Ruemu asked Ogaga,

'Do you have twenty thousand naira? The driver said it is thirty-five thousand naira, and I've only got ten thousand naira. I have to go inside the house and get some money,' Ogaga said. He walked back through the front gate and then returned with a wad of twenty thousand naira which he handed to Ruemu, who took out five thousand naira, pocketed fifteen thousand naira, then handed twenty-five thousand naira to the driver.

'Ogaga, I was thinking we could keep this driver; he brought me all the way from the airport and he is a very good driver.' He pointed to a dark plumpish lady who sat on the other side of the car. 'My friend unfortunately got us lost. That is why it took us so long to get here.'

'Let me go and ask Mum what she thinks.' Ochuko had returned about half an hour before Ruemu had arrived.

Ruemu had told the driver to wait outside and followed Ogaga into the house to speak to Ochuko. 'Mum, I've got a driver here. I was thinking he could take us around for the period of this burial, it would make life a lot easier while we are here.'

'That's a very good idea; it would save us being at the mercy of others and means we don't have to wait for your aunty to come back before we go out,' Ochuko said.

Peter went back outside. 'Dennis, *sey you fi follow stay for the next three days?*'

'Let me ask my oga,' the driver said. He brought a small black phone from his pocket, dialled a number and put it to his ear. 'Oga, the passenger I picked up wants me to stay with them. Is this OK with you? We have agreed a price of twenty thousand naira a day.'

With the price agreed and Dennis's oga accepting the

request to hire his vehicle, Ruemu said to Ogaga, 'It is better for all of us, otherwise he would be going to the airport every day to hustle for rides. On some days he might not even get anybody to take because of the competition.'

Ochuko promptly decided they should go to Kokori to see how far the preparations had gone. After they unloaded Ruemu's belongings, they all got into the seven-seater, and Ochuko directed Dennis to late Pa Otutu's compound in Kokori.

An Evening with the Elders

When they had arrived at the compound in Kokori, the group disembarked from the car. The sight before them was very disheartening. The house that Kevwe had been charged to refurbish stood before them. Ogaga and Ruemu's older brother Kevwe had told them that Pa Otutu, on his dying bed, had charged him with completing the house in Kokori that he started.

It was a large house which had been raised to roofing level, with holes in the sides for windows but no windows. It had one light at the side of it facing the road. Right in front of the house was debris—lots and lots of debris—consisting of sand, rocks, dried cement, and pieces of wood that could be presumed to be waste.

He had apparently said, 'Kevwe, make sure you finish the house. That is where I will be buried.' This is the explanation that Kevwe gave for refusing his younger siblings' advice and Ochuko's advice to beg the elders of their dad's village to allow them to bury him in his other house, where some of his relatives were currently staying.

In Urhobo culture the dying wish of a man is regarded to

be as immutable as natural laws. If this were truly one of his last words, then this is what they should have done regardless of cost. Ogaga, however, remembered that fateful night when he got the call from Ese: one of his older siblings.

It was Friday 17 June. Ogaga had just returned from work, when his phone rang; a Nigerian number was displayed on the screen. As far as Ogaga could remember, good news doesn't usually come from Nigeria. 'Hello Ogaga,' he said. He heard sobbing on the phone.

'Ogaga, *Ose gwu ni re* (daddy has died). They took him from us. It will not be well with them. Apparently, he had gone to sleep and never woke up again.' This was after about two days of being readmitted in the hospital. Ogaga couldn't imagine when Pa Otutu would have given this dying wish.

As the company surveyed the massive compound that had belonged to Pa Otutu, they were awed by how big it was, but perplexed about the lack of evidence that there was a funeral here. The door to the house was locked, there was a heap of sand outside the house, and there was a smaller heap of gravel and wood in front of the house.

There were only four canopies right at the back of the compound, which Ochuko had paid for to be set up for the family. There were only a few chairs by the side of the wall. There was a topless young man sitting by the front door of the house. Ochuko called to him, 'Come here, what are you doing here?' The topless young man, whose dark skin was covered with dust, appeared to have been working in the sun.

'I am waiting for my money.'

'Who owes you money?'

The topless man replied, 'The one they call Kevwe.'

'How much?'

'One thousand naira,' the young man responded. 'He asked me to dig the hole in the side there, and he hasn't come back to pay me.' So it appeared that this young man was a grave digger—well, at least for a few hours he was.

Ogaga and Ruemu were so aghast at the situation that they started clearing the front of the house. They offered the topless young man work if he would help them clear the area in preparation for tomorrow. They would pay him a further one thousand naira. After about thirty minutes of working, a skinny elderly man in an Urhobo kaftan staggered into the compound.

He stood at a small distance from Ogaga and his company, put his hand on his chin and started laughing. 'My children, it is enough, leave that, leave it alone.' Ruemu put away his makeshift shovel which was a piece of flatwood that he had been using to move dirt and rocks. Ogaga was using a long piece of wood to do the same and picking up big rocks, which he deposited in a new heap they were creating at the side of the house where they imagined there would be no guests.

The young man had galvanised four small boys who had hired two wheelbarrows and two shovels, and were also moving dirt and debris, dumping it by the side of the house away from where most of the event would take place. The group was about to start moving the sand in front of the house, when the old man came forward and greeted Ochuko, who acknowledged him as Amos.

'My children, leave the sand, it can be used to fill the grave tomorrow.' This was the first time that Ogaga and Ruemu had met their Uncle Amos: he was their dad's younger cousin. He had an interesting walk: he sort of staggered with every step that he took.

Ochuko introduced him. 'This is your Uncle Amos.'

'*Miguo uncle*,' chorused Ogaga and Ruemu.

'*Owa vren* (get up guys).' Ochuko's sons had bowed their knees when greeting him as was customary when greeting elders in Urhobo culture. People were often surprised they understood Urhobo and could speak it.

'Amos,' Ochuko called to him, 'so what is happening with this burial? We came here to see what preparations had been made for the funeral. And here we are, nothing has been set up. When I came here three days ago, the place was overgrown with grass up to my shoulder; I had to pay people to cut all the grass.'

Ochuko had paid fifty thousand naira for the grass to be cut, as the compound was extremely large.

'Don't worry, my dear, it would hold, listen to what I'm saying, listen to what I'm saying!' Amos chorused gregariously and loudly, almost as if people had come for a different event.

Danger in Sapele

Today was a big day for the Kawere gang. Captain had heard of English Christian missionaries living in Sapele. From his sources, they had been there for the last four months. The missionaries were here doing medical missions; two of them were doctors. Captain could already see the dollar signs; more correctly the pound signs, these were high profile targets.

This was the Kawere gang's main hustle. They spent weeks planning such kidnappings and ransom negotiations. Everything had to be right. You needed spotters that blended in with the surroundings at the drop-off points; you needed trustworthy informants who loved the power of money.

The Kawere gang had a side hustle: they were kidnappers,

period. So they also made small chops, as Captain called it, on kidnapping children, infants, women for sex trafficking, child slavery and ritual sacrifice. He himself didn't believe in the ritual sacrifices. If it worked, why was there so much poverty around? He was a profiteer; wherever there was money to be made.

Well, the work has to begin. They would need to wrap up this job pretty quickly just before these missionaries were due to leave.

Mr Yakubu picked up *The Punch* newspaper—his favourite newspaper. Every morning he picked up the Nigerian *Punch*. It helped him keep abreast of the pulse in Nigeria; what was actually happening, what people actually thought of the political elite. Many of the other newspapers over-indulged in brown envelope journalism. Writing whatever celebrities and politicians paid them to write.

The Nigerian *Punch*

Four British aid workers have been kidnapped in broad daylight in Delta state, Nigeria. The team had been out there doing medical missionary work for the last four months. The Kawere gang has claimed responsibility. A ransom demand has been made to the British High Commission in Nigeria.

Mr Yakubu smiled, picked up his phone and dialled; on the second ring Captain picked up.

'I see your work; I see dollars are falling from the sky again.'

'It hasn't dropped yet, we are just waiting for the *oyinbo* people to drop lunch money. You know how difficult these things are. You are too big for this kind of thing.'

'Don't talk that one; you know say, *na condition wey*

make crayfish bend.'

'*Na true sha*, hopefully manna will fall from heaven soon.'

'I called to congratulate you in advance and to let you know I might have a job for you.'

Captain sighed and concluded by saying noted, after a brief discussion on the proposed job.

The line went dead.

Yakubu imagined the headline in the *Punch*. *Local philanthropist, Mr Yakubu, elected to the seat of councillor in Ulomo district, Lagos.*

Chapter Twelve

Two by two, turn by turn

'Ese!' barked Ben, 'bring the money out; let's pay the driver.' The three brothers were just about to charter a taxi from the motor park in Ojota, Lagos. Kevwe and Ese planted themselves in the rear of the vehicle; their luggage fitted snugly into the back of the black Toyota Auris they had just gotten into. Ben sat himself in the front seat. They had decided they wanted the vehicle all to themselves. It was a five-seater vehicle.

Normally, the driver would have waited for one more passenger, calling out his fare, '*Warri, Warri, ewole* (enter those travelling to Warri).' It is usual for Nigerians to shout the same things over and over again; this was the fairly standard way of attracting clients onto public transport. They repeated their phrases for several reasons: to stop passengers from entering the wrong vehicle and, secondly, to make sure they were heard in the midst of the usual raucous.

Ese replied in a very gentle manner. 'Don't worry, I have.' Turning to the driver, 'I'll pay you when we get to our destination. *Melo ni*? (how much is it?)' he asked in the unofficial second language of Lagos state.

'Twenty thousand naira,' the driver beamed.

Kevwe piped in. 'Driver, that is daylight robbery. The individual fare is normally about four to five thousand naira each.'

The driver said, 'I'm even giving you cheap, *abi* you are hiring the vehicle, and I'm taking you to the hotel in Warri, which we have to find when we reach Warri, no be so.'

Ben interjected. 'Twenty thousand naira is OK, let's just go. It is only three days to the burial date, and there are a lot of things on ground that we have to sort out.' He closed the passenger side door. The driver started off his rusty black Toyota Auris, which coughed healthily to life. He pressed on the accelerator while not in gear, and in response a roaring noise bellowed from the engine along with a plume of black smoke.

When you see the black plumes and smoke that come from vehicles in Nigeria, you would wonder if any of them were fitted with catalytic converters.

He switched into gear and began the process of navigating his way out of the motor park. He moved slowly, but aggressively, through the crowd of people—a feat most Nigerian drivers could manage—revving the engine and coming right up behind people's knees without hitting the persons. Hawkers selling meat pie, plantain chips, pure water, and gala scrambled out of the way. Unfortunately, one hawker had dropped an alleged pair of designer glasses he was selling as the driver was just exiting the park. And although the hawker jumped out of the way in time, the alleged glasses didn't make it and suffered under the tyres of the Toyota.

The car spun out of the car park, entering the road, starting to make a beeline towards Obanikoro and Anthony. It joined the third mainland bridge, which is the longest of three bridges connecting Lagos Island to the mainland. It ploughed slowly but steadily through the traffic, typical Lagos traffic. In truth, it wasn't so bad at present. It was moving, which was a good sign; they would soon be out of Lagos and the traffic would improve. They entered Shagamu onto the express road and were well on their way.

The brothers had all been in terrible traffic in Lagos multiple times especially during rush hour. At times it could take ten minutes to move every two hundred yards in the Lagos traffic. Forty-five minutes later they were out of Lagos, heading towards Ogun state. Three hours later they were in Warri. It didn't prove that difficult to locate their hotel.

They arrived at the premises of Lawfab Hotel after disembarking from the taxi. Ese paid the driver. The brothers then proceeded in for check in to the hotel. The porters helped with their luggage and showed them to their rooms. Ben was staying in a standard room by himself, while Ese and Kevwe decided to share a room.

The three brothers gathered in Ben's room for their first meeting at four pm Wednesday afternoon. 'So where do we start?' Ben began.

'I don't know how this is all going to happen,' Kevwe began. 'We still haven't bought the cow, and the burial is only two days away. I tried to get hold of Ogaga and all he told me over the phone was that he will join us when he gets to Nigeria, so I think he is arriving tomorrow. However, I've used some of the money to buy a bag of rice, a bag of beans and a tin of oil. We will have to cook it in Papa's compound.'

Ese piped in. 'That means we will need to hire cooks as well as a gas cooker. There is a problem, there will be nowhere to store the food.'

'Well, the food will be cooked on the same day starting in the late morning, so the timing should be just about right to serve,' Kevwe said.

'Do you think this will be enough for everybody?' Ben asked.

'We are doing our best. It is Ogaga and Ruemu that are messing up. At least Ruemu has tried. Ogaga is acting very strange, almost like it is nothing to do with him. I think it is their mother; she is turning them against us. If not for her, this whole process would be going much smoother.'

'You know I said to him the other day, how can you contribute just five hundred thousand naira for your father's burial,' Kevwe said. He didn't mention to them the part where Ogaga responded with saying aside from Ruemu he had contributed more than everyone, and he remembered he wasn't meant to be contributing to the building process in the first instance.

'Irhorho called me while we were in the car,' Ese said. 'She is now in Delta state; she is staying at her friend's place, Bronhe. She should be here in the next hour to pick up the materials and our measurements and take it to the tailor for us. I've got the money for that here. And, Ben, what about the money I gave to you for the drinks for the elders during the ceremony?' Ben coughed and started to say… 'There was a slight problem, there was some running around I needed to do and the people cheated me. So, I wasn't able to get the drinks and kolanuts.'

In his mind he recollected going to Naijabet to try to double the money. It had been about three years now since he had been visiting the betting shop. He had been pursuing his music career up until recently, now being forty-seven years of age. The monies he had been receiving were his opportunity to quadruple the amount so that he could have enough to buy some equipment and studio time to rejuvenate his music career.

Two decades ago, he was the future of Nigerian hiplife music. His debut single had played in all Nigerian radio stations and media outlets. Coming out as the artist known as 'DMOne'. As it often happened in Nigeria, it was about who you knew, and after performing at many events and recording a few other songs, it took him about a year before he realised that the powers that be in the music industry had no intention of pushing him forward. One of the tracks he wrote was even stolen and given to another now famous and world-renowned Nigerian hiplife star. This guy now collaborates with American hip-hop stars.

Ben was confident of his talent; fast forward over thirty years and he was going to prove them wrong. He was going to blow! Naijabet opening in the last few years presented him with another opportunity to produce his own album, and then bring it to the right people. His forage into Naijabet started three years ago when he first started accompanying Pa Otutu to Kokori. Pa Otutu had decided to sell the house in Mile Twelve. He saw himself retiring back in the village.

Ben was in charge of Pa Otutu's money, as his eyesight was poor due to glaucoma from diabetes which he had suffered with for many years now. Ben had access to Pa Otutu's money and accounts on this trip; this enabled Ben's lifestyle of women and time in the studio to be funded.

He had repaid this in full. He was the one who sat with Pa Otutu during his hospital stay. He cleaned him, assisted him to the toilet, looked out for him, and kept him company. He also dealt with the family lawyer who was dealing with the legal battle regarding the house in Lagos.

'Those two, especially Ogaga, do not realise just how expensive things are in Nigeria,' Ben said. 'Ogaga is so ungrateful; after all I've done for them. I asked them to make contributions and they ignored me.' Ben saw himself as the man responsible for getting Ogaga and Ruemu to London for the first time. When their mum had come to pick them, as she had previously agreed with Pa Otutu the first time, Pa Otutu wasn't home and Ben, being in the position of the eldest male in the house, said they should go and shouldn't wait for Pa Otutu.

Besides, Pa Otutu could be contentious, even though he had said his children could go and live with their mum in London, it would not have been a surprise to see him change his mind in the last few minutes. What Pa Otutu said to two different people wasn't always exactly the same thing. Ben even accompanied them on their way to the airport.

Kevwe then added, 'What baffles me is the rudeness that Ogaga displays; he is meant to be a Christian. Then he acts like this. He forgets we are his elders and he is supposed to do what we tell him.'

'Maybe he really doesn't have money,' Ese said.

'Don't give me that nonsense,' Ben snapped! 'Anyhow, let us put our heads together to figure out how we are going to get out of this mess. We haven't bought the casket yet, even the cloth Daddy needs to be clothed in hasn't been bought, the cow is still missing, and what about the canopies?'

'Well, I'll go and meet a man today to secure the musicians that will be singing and to pay for eleven canopies, and two hundred chairs,' Kevwe said. 'Hopefully, Ogaga should be calling either today or tomorrow, then we will have the three hundred thousand naira we need for the cow. Right now, all the money we have left over is six hundred thousand naira.'

'And that is to cover our hotel bill, funeral expenses and transport back to Lagos,' said Ese. Ese sighed, this was followed by sighs from Kevwe and Ben. Kevwe got up, walked to the window and pulled the curtains back, letting in some sunlight even though the lights in the hotel room had been on. It was afternoon still and there was plenty of sunlight. He opened the windows because the room felt so stuffy and hot. The heat was getting to them; they had done well to get so far against all the underhanded dealings of the village elders, but he wasn't sure they could cross the finishing line.

The three in the room were all in this together, but it wasn't a very nice meeting. Deep down, there was a fear in each one of them that they didn't have the resources or organisational to pull this burial off. It was something they wouldn't admit, but they were waiting for Ogaga and Ruemu. Their plea for funds from the rest of the children had largely gone unheeded. Victoria's children had in total contributed fifty thousand naira between the four of them. Even though they were the youngest, they were all in their early to late twenties.

Igho had contributed nothing, he had talked a good talk. Anyway, Kevwe had spoken to him just before the meeting, and he had arrived that morning from Abuja to Kokori. Whether he liked it or not, he would be paying the sixty-five thousand naira to get the coffin. It would be his contribution. When Kevwe thought about it, Ben had contributed nothing financially to this burial process. He had summoned meetings and barked orders. His trips to Delta state to meet with the elders and prepare as necessary for this occasion wasn't funded from his pocket, but from the money they had received from Choja, Ruemu and Ogaga in London.

Kevwe himself had contributed four hundred thousand naira to the cause. Ese had contributed a similar amount besides the expenses he had borne himself and not told anybody about. Kevwe felt he had done as best a job with the hand he was dealt; he had been the go-to man, the action man. He spent a month in Kokori getting the house in Pa Otutu's compound ready. Leaving his wife and three children in Lagos, of course he had to give them some feeding money from the money he received. At one point, things were so bad that he got stuck in Warri; he made several calls until Ruemu sent him some money to enable him to leave Warri for Lagos state.

He had stayed in this very hotel on his previous visits, it had fast become an unwelcome home away from home. He hated being here, but he had always come back ever since this fateful proceeding began. He hated the blandness of the hotel; he disliked the relative quietness in contrast to the business of Lagos; he missed his family and his own bed. In a very strange way, he missed his father. He couldn't understand why a lot of the children were behaving this way, especially the younger ones. Dad never did anything to them or mistreated them. This was not necessarily a fact. This was what Kevwe thought at the time, and whenever he thought something it fast became a fact.

'Kevwe, Kevwe!' He heard Ese and Ben call his name simultaneously. He had no idea how long he had been staring at the traffic on the streets below; they were on the first floor. He dragged his feet back to where his two other brothers were sitting, and he resumed his seat. There was one wooden armchair which Ben sat in. Ese and Kevwe had been sitting on the edges of the single bed.

As he sat down, Ben's phone rang. 'Hello, who is this?'

'It is Irhorho, I'm at the hotel, what's the room number?'

'Come to room 118 on the first floor.'

Irhorho knocked on room 118. Ese opened the door for her as she ran in screaming, embracing each of her brothers in return. 'It is so good to see all of you.'

Kevwe and Ese smiled at her. 'You are a very silly girl,' Kevwe said endearingly. He looked at her with a scowl. 'How can you be behaving like this at a time like this? You should have been here a while ago so we can put heads together to sort out this issue on ground.'

'How are you?' Ese asked.

'I am blessed and highly favoured,' she beamed loudly. She had a backpack on, and was also holding a nylon bag with some containers.

'Brother Ben, Brother Ben,' she said repeatedly in a playful manner. She moved to his side and started to tickle him and they both started laughing. 'You know how it is. I'm always rejoicing and we have every reason to be happy, it is not every day that we gather together. And I'll be seeing the others as well. I heard Aunty Anna is here. Have Ruemu and Ogaga arrived? Also, Ochuko told me they are on the road and will be arriving in the village at Kokori tonight.'

'So back to business,' Ese motioned. 'Irhorho, the money that you were allocated to contribute, you didn't contribute it. Of the two hundred and fifty thousand naira, you promised sixty thousand naira six months ago, and we are yet to see a kobo.'

'My brothers, I'm sorry but the truth is that I don't have anything, even coming here was a challenge. I can only try. Also, I'm staying at my friend's place, and she will be coming with me to the burial.'

'That's enough, Irhorho.' Kevwe gestured for her to be quiet. 'What about the other matter we talked about? The responsibility we have given you.'

'I'm ready to go!' Irhorho removed the strap of the backpack she had been carrying. She was wearing blue jeans and a purple top with pearl beads sewn to the top half of the top in spiral patterns. She rested the backpack on the floor, crouched down and opening the zip, brought out a small folder.

'This is it,' she said. 'I've drawn diagrams of what the male outfit is supposed to look like and also what the female attire is going to look like. I've also got a few pictures on my phone from the internet on what it is going to look like. Brother Ese, it is lace that you bought isn't it? Then you bought George material as well. The combination you chose is a beautiful combination: white lace top with silver George wrapper.' Irhorho flashed her phone in the faces of her brothers, showing the images she had downloaded off Google, with dark-skinned people dressed in various colours of the same style. The men had black top hats, brightly coloured lace tops and George wrappers tied around their waists.

Many of the tribes in the Delta region tied wrappers. In the olden days they used a rope or piece of string to secure it. This was often obscured by the wrapper folded over it, and nowadays men tended to use a belt below the wrapper.

'All I need now is the money. I've got the measurements for everyone: I got Ben's, Ese's, Kevwe's, Anna's and Igho's measurements.' The numbers didn't add up. Kevwe handed over thirty thousand naira from the bunch in his hand; it was from the money that had been deposited in his account by Ruemu. There was, however, no outfit being sewn for Ruemu or many of the other children. All they knew was that the colour of the day was white.

'I'm going to start going now. Onajevwe said she will come from Uncle Amos's house later today. I'll see all of you tomorrow. I have to get to the tailor now. Also, I've to meet Bronhe to take me to her. Before I forget, I cooked this beautiful ogwuoeri soup for you guys; you can get some garri or starch to eat it with.' She handed the plastic bag to Ben, whose face beamed with joy. 'I'll see you all tomorrow, love you.' Irhorho said, as she left the room. Ese and Kevwe's eyes wandered from the closed door until they rested their eyes on Ben again, who seemed lost in thought with his hands in his head.

Chapter Thirteen

Kevwe

Kevwe was actually a twin child; his twin brother was stillborn. He was a miracle child. He was one of the most popular and cool kids among Pa Otutu's children. Growing up, his sense of humour and his deep caring for everyone were always there to be seen. He walked into the rooms of the different wives and their children without restraint; he saw everyone as his brother and sister and treated them all the same.

However, it became evident to Ogaga that Kevwe had a problem with money. Ogaga remembered when he was ten years old, around twenty years ago. One day he had one hundred naira, during this period one hundred naira was a significant amount of money. If you wound the clock another twenty years before that time, one naira was equivalent to a British pound.

Kevwe asked Ogaga to loan him the hundred naira; Kevwe promised to pay it back the following week. The following week came but the hundred naira didn't come. Ogaga waited a whole month before giving up on the money. It would be another two years before Ogaga would leave the family home for London.

Ogaga recalled several incidents. He had agreed to go into business with Kevwe. He had purchased a number of mobile handsets from a wholesaler in the UK whom he had sourced online. Kevwe had been on his case about this, as he was adamant he could sell them, for more than fifty percent of the price Ogaga purchased them for.

The phones were shipped to Lagos, and Kevwe called to ask for money to clear the phones from customs. He was supposed to bring a return of investment within two months. Within a month, he had sold four phones which people had paid for, he had decided to give two away as a gift, keep one for himself, and the remainder of the phones people had taken with a promise to pay shortly. According to Kevwe those funds never arrived. Ogaga couldn't understand how someone who was trying to go into the supply business for mobile phones couldn't move twenty phones. That was an investment lost.

Skipping down a decade, Kevwe called Ogaga again. He had been bugging him prior to this with regards to investing in his diamond business and oil business. Apparently Kevwe now had licenses to trade in oil and to sell diamonds overseas.

He made a trip to Dubai to strike a deal to sell some gemstones for an interested party in Nigeria. He checked into a hotel and waited several days for a meeting with a gemstone specialist. The specialist never arrived and the meeting never took place. Kevwe faced being thrown in prison in the United Arab Emirates, so he made his ten phone calls to Ogaga, crying and pleading for him to pay for his hotel stay, which Ogaga paid for with his debit card. The next day Kevwe boarded the plane back to Nigeria, no contract in hand, no money in his account.

There were many more stories like this. It all starts with the latest business idea and the guarantee that this is going to work. When Ogaga thought about it, Kevwe never had a business plan. Ogaga wasn't even sure he knew how to write a business plan. After many years of giving Kevwe the benefit of the doubt, the little trust and willingness to sacrifice was lost on Ogaga.

Like Ochuko always said to Ogaga, nothing in Nigeria ever works, no amount of money you pour into a project reaps useful benefit. It felt like the land was under a curse. People tried to pull others around them down, but they would pander to the politicians and rich crooks who are responsible for the situation where the majority of the people are—those who are below the breadline.

Brrringg! Brrringg! What was that sound? Oke turned over in bed, coming face to face with her phone. Her younger sister was still sleeping. She picked up the phone; the caller ID showed Kevwe's name. She groaned out loud. 'What now? It is seven am.' Not that seven am was particularly early, but they had arrived Thursday evening, and up untill now hadn't been told what time the funeral was meant to be starting.

'Hello, *Miguo bros*, how are you?'

'I'm fine,' Kevwe responded. 'Oke! Tell Efe, Ochuko and Loretta we need more funds. We are going to bury Daddy today, we must bury Daddy! What we need now is money to get the body from the mortuary. I have to say this has been disgraceful. You know your father hasn't done anything against any of you. It was us, the older ones, he maltreated, yet none of you have contributed anything significant. It is disgraceful.'

'Bros please! I'm sorry to say, but what you are saying is

not helpful; we are here to bury our father. Let me speak to my siblings. We will meet you at the compound. What time should we meet you? Then whatever we can afford we will give to you.'

'OK, if you say so, bye.' Kevwe responded.

Oke was upset. It was a feeling of irritation the younger ones were becoming accustomed to, after meeting or speaking with the older children of the house, since Pa Otutu passed.

Oke thought rhetorically that all he ever did was ask. Well, he was living up to his name, for if you translated the abbreviated name Kevwe, literally it meant 'give me'. The full name was Oghenekevwe; which meant 'this is what God has given me'.

It was the morning of the funeral, or at least supposed to be. The result of this phone call woke everybody up as they got ready. Everyone had a bath, and they all had breakfast around about eleven am. At eleven forty-five am they were all at Pa Otutu's compound. The only person they saw there was Aunty Onajevwe. Ruemu and Ogaga arrived fifteen minutes later; they had no clue what time the funeral was meant to begin. Aunty Onajevwe was the eldest girl child of Pa Otutu, but they called her aunty because she was older than them.

An Impasse

'If today is tomorrow, there will be no yesterday'

Back in the compound in Kokori, the Bakasi boys had set up an impasse at where the gate should have been, as they banged on the ambulance. 'Saying over my dead body will this body enter here'. Ruemu, Ogaga and their mother watched the scene before them from beneath the canopies; Ruemu and Ogaga were both standing, hands in pockets, seething openly with anger. Over by the corner of the house were their elder brothers and some of their sisters. The oldest son sat on a chair with his head in his hands.

He was the oldest son but not the first born: the first born had died some twenty years ago in a motor vehicle accident. Ogaga had seen it happen in a dream he told one of his brothers. The next day after telling his dream, messengers came to his father's house in Lagos bearing the grievous news. And Pa Otutu sat on his chair, beat his chest and wailed just as Ogaga had seen in his dream.

The annex had specifically been built to be a resting place for Pa Otutu. It was a room with a rectangular hole in the middle of the floor, long and wide enough to put a coffin in. This, traditionally, was how all great Urhobo people are to be buried. There is an Urhobo saying, 'When someone has lived a good life, you do not leave them outside for the rain to beat them'. For this reason, they bury notable individuals in houses, usually in an annex room.

When Ogaga had visited Pa Otutu's compound the day before, the annex gate was locked. It was a black gate with a padlock on it. What surprised him was how little several millions of naira could buy in this village in Nigeria. The total that had been contributed to building this house was over six million. It was a seven-bedroom house. Before the decision had been made to refurbish it, it was already standing raised to roof level. With no plastering, no windows or doors, however, it had the form of a house. Kevwe, one of his brothers had received instruction from Pa Otutu to complete this house, apparently on his dying bed.

He had plastered the whole house, but not the floors, and the 'suck away', important for drainage of sewage wasn't complete. Even on that evening when they had come, it wasn't even covered. It was filled with rain water. It made one wonder if Kevwe understood Pa Otutu's request to complete the house.

There was a solitary neon LED light on the side of the house facing the road; obviously the electrics weren't connected. It was abysmal that six million naira had been spent on developing this house, when people have been known to build houses from scratch for 2 million naira. It certainly wasn't habitable. He wasn't impressed by the outward appearance of the exterior either; there was no gate at the main entrance.

What was impressive was the sheer size of the property: it was about the size of six football pitches and the house only occupied about one football pitch. It was impressive standing in the compound. They had been expecting to see the older children that evening, but they were nowhere to be found, and when they called them, they said they were in Warri having a meeting in their hotel.

Pa Otutu had been a man who had built many houses. He had another house in Kokori which he had built for his parents; some of his kinsmen and relatives currently occupied that house. There was the house where he was to be buried; he had built a house there many moons ago. However, a few years ago he had thought to retire to the village. So, he had torn down the old building that had been on the site and started constructing this house in the large compound. In his younger days he had built a house that then sank into the ground, and the government ended up seizing that land. What he seemed to have built more than anything were children as evidenced today.

There was a scripture from the Psalms known to Ogaga,

which talked about the blessedness of the man who had many children; that they are like arrows in the hands of a mighty man; that would allow him to speak with the enemy at the gates.

Not all of his children were coming to the funeral. There was one in Australia, another in Canada, and another one who lived in Lagos, Nigeria. There had been two who had died. Pa Otutu's first born had died in his thirties in a car accident; however, his eldest son and the first grandson were here. No one was really sure exactly how many children he had. At a time, he was married to six wives at the peak of his powers; this was beside concubines and girlfriend. Most of the children thought he had about 25 children, with a few children discovered along the way. No one could speak about the ones that were not discovered, or even the girlfriends that weren't discovered. The wives were known because these were the ones for whom he paid their bride price.

Around the corner from the compound was parked a blue Toyota Auris, a thin topless man sat in the driver seat. The engine was off and the doors were open. It was hot, evidenced by the fact the driver had taken off his shirt and was reclining backwards in the driver's seat, with a sachet of cold iced water pressed to his lips. His passenger wasn't with him. The driver had nosed the car into the little side street where it couldn't be seen by anyone in the compound per chance.

The passenger of the blue Toyota Auris was a dark man dressed in green work trousers and a khaki green shirt. He stood on the opposite side of the road, among the onlookers, facing the entrance to the compound. There were many onlookers, that itself wasn't abnormal. People always knew when something was going to happen.

This was because people would often invite themselves to all parties, so that they could be fed. The village people had seen very little in terms of posters indicating the start time all they knew was it was on Saturday. So obviously there were the unofficial spies who lived close by and would pass the message on as soon as the party got going.

Yakubu watched in bemusement, as he hid among the crowd of onlookers. Today he had time, he had come for the sole purpose of finding out if his defeat was absolute. He had wondered after the judge read out the verdict in his civil case against the family of the deceased, whether Pa Otutu had snatched victory from him in death. He hoped he could take back what belonged to him and hopefully more, regardless that Pa Otutu had moved on. He was the shrewd man and couldn't bear to lose.

He hoped he might hear something, or better yet, find someone. He had long since cut his acquaintance with Modupe; she hadn't delivered, and he had allowed her to go back to her poverty-stricken life. When the idea for the trip came about, he called her promising her the opportunity to make some money, in his words salvage victory from the jaws of defeat. She was seated in the back of the car at present; he had warned her not to come out.

The spectacle before him was entertaining. He smirked outwardly, but laughed inwardly that Pa Otutu might not get buried. Even if nothing else was to come of this trip, this might in itself justify the two hundred miles he had come from Lagos to try to recover some of his losses. Although he had a couple of other business matters and loose ends to tie up in this area.

Chapter Fourteen

The morning of the burial

'The sky is grey but there is no rain, the rain must come sometime'

Today was the morning of the burial; no one knew what was going to happen. Even on the sparse posters advertising to the local community that the funeral ceremony of the late Pa Otutu was taking place, no starting time had been placed on the event. Clearly, from the day before, the older children had not made adequate preparations. Ruemu and Ogaga had turned to the wisdom of their mother, Ochuko; the same one who had cleared the grass. She had also hired five canopies for the family and paid for food to feed fifty people. A sparse number compared to the crowd of five hundred that the older brothers had written into their budget.

One of Ogaga's concerns on seeing the budget they had sent him while he was in London was how the budget had changed. The first budget totalled at about 3.6 million naira and didn't include the expenses of the house. The new budget, sent a few months earlier, was around five million naira, and didn't include things such as food, the cost of paying the mortuary bills or for the ambulance to bring the corpse to the compound.

Ogaga mused on these thoughts as he got ready. His wife had already showered and gotten dressed. It had come to this, that she would only meet her father in-law in death. That only conversation she had with him nineteen months ago ended up being the only conversation she had with him. Ogaga was having difficulty fitting his outfit, which involved tying a yellow wrapper. A long and wide piece of yellow material, the ends of which he held, spread his feet wide and wound a knot round his waist. He then folded the knot into itself, and underneath the wrapper. In truth, the knot was tied around his chest rather than his waist. Not that he was short, but the wrapper was quite long. He linked a belt underneath the knot to hold it in position.

The colour of the day was supposed to be all white, but Ogaga had stopped caring; the thing he cared least about at the moment, was to blend in with everyone, especially his so-called siblings. He and his wife basically picked something they already had, the wrappers were donated by his mum and the tops, which were green, were donated by his uncle from the United States. At least he matched with his wife and they looked regal in their attire. He walked out of the room calling, 'Ruemu, are you ready?' No answer. After walking to the adjacent room, he banged on the door to which his older brother replied 'yes', he was clearly still in bed. It was already about nine thirty in the morning. However, Ruemu also got up and proceeded to get ready.

'Mum, what time are we supposed to go for this funeral? I messaged my brothers yesterday but no one has responded,' Ogaga asked.

Ochuko responded, 'Who knows if they will show up?

You guys should go there for twelve pm to make sure everything is ready; besides we can't go anywhere due to the environmental curfew.' It was Saturday, and it was sanitation day, essentially movement by car was restricted until people had done some tidying of their local environment.

As they clambered into the seven-seater Sienna vehicle, they had a look of amusement on their faces; no one really knew how bad the day was going to go. 'This is ridiculous,' Ruemu said, 'don't poor people bury their dead, and why is this so disorganised? Seriously, those brothers of yours deserve a whooping.'

'They're your brothers,' retorted Ogaga. Dennis drove quietly today; even his small black phone which usually rang intermittently, as his boss called to check on him, was silent, as the vehicle left Okpara—their mother's village—to make the twenty-minute journey to Kokori.

The first stop was to drop their mum and Ogaga's wife off at an uncle's place in Kokori, he happened to be one of the chiefs of the village. The next stop was to their father's compound. The two young men sat apprehensively for the three-minute journey to the compound. After Dennis had dropped them off, he pulled into a neat rather large alcove by the side of the house, flung his doors wide open, and reclined the driver's seat till it was horizontal. He walked out of the compound to get some pure water, then reclined in the vehicle. He possibly sensed that today was going to be a long day.

Ruemu and Ogaga, on exiting the vehicle, looked around for anything familiar. Things were a bit different from when they were here last night. There was a white canopy to their immediate right, and under it, being set up, were speakers and microphones. There was a small group of people in uniforms, which were made from brown and yellow Ankara material, which the brothers guessed were the musicians.

Directly opposite them there were young men putting up canopies, and they were starting to form a line, it appeared there probably would be twelve all along the left side of the large compound. There were now several stacks of white plastic chairs underneath these canopies waiting to be put out.

Several traders selling food and groceries and soft drinks had set up tables and spread their wares in plain sight, just outside and at the mouth of the compound. A few young men with cameras around their necks pranced around; their cameras looked like one of those cameras that printed out instant photos the moment they were shot. They would invariably charge for this.

From the description you might be inclined to think that somebody with extraordinary organisational skills had taken pains and gone to great length to make this a day beneficial for everyone. Fortunately, or unfortunately, depending who you were, it wasn't so. It wasn't the way it was, it was just the way things worked; people heard some kind of party was happening today, and the compound had now become a marketplace.

In the Compound
'We are in the compound, come and play, don't enter if you are here to fight'

When they arrived in the compound, they saw some of their younger siblings sitting and standing around in the porch, then they saw Onajevwe, the eldest daughter of their father. She approached them and after greeting her, they said, 'Sister, do you know what is happening? Where is everybody? We've been unable to get hold of Kevwe and Ben.'

'Well, they all went to collect the coffin from the mortuary this morning, and as for Kevwe, he is on his way from Warri.'

She went on to say, 'We have a big problem on ground.' She didn't need to finish her sentence. The forlorn expression on her face told it all.

'Unfortunately, the cow we were hoping to use died on the way here, so we need to get another cow for today, so that we can start cooking and feed everyone.' Ogaga and Ruemu looked at their watches. Ruemu walked off and started talking to some of his younger siblings. Ogaga said, 'How is this possible? It is twelve-thirty pm. How are we going to find a cow, kill the cow then prepare everything for it to be ready in time? You know it takes all day to prepare a cow.'

To which she replied, 'My brother, what can I do? Let us first go and buy the cow.'

Normally, when people are doing celebrations in Nigeria, the cow is bought within two to three days of the event, and usually either slaughtered the day before to start preparations, or at worse very early in the morning; so the dressers could get to work, followed by the cooks who would start cooking a few hours later. It takes a long time when you are cooking for a large crowd.

'It doesn't make any sense to me. What about getting a goat or even chicken, which is much quicker to cook?'

His sister replied, 'I don't know, let me ask Uncle Amos first.'

Uncle Amos happened to be passing by, and after asking him, he replied, 'Whatever you have is acceptable.' Goats and fish were on the budget. Ogaga wasn't sure if all the goats escaped or the fishes swam back into the ocean out of the budget sheet.

Ogaga then asked, 'How much do you need?'

She then replied, 'Come with me to Ugheli to the market where we can buy the turkey.'

Ogaga replied, 'Let me think about it first, because the driver needs to go and pick my mum, can't take him now.' He walked off and after speaking with Ruemu came back and said, 'I can't come with you, I need to be here.' The interesting thing about the issue was that the kitchen was non-functional, and there would have been nowhere to prepare food.

'I will go and prepare it in Uncle Amos's house, and then bring the food back here.'

'How?' Ogaga enquired. 'That is something that should have been done this morning.'

'Well, I wasn't given any money, I hoped your older brothers would give me money to do the cooking, but up untill now I have received nothing.'

When Ogaga greeted his younger siblings, they informed him that some said the cow had jumped out of the vehicle on the way to Delta and had gotten lost, whereas others claimed the cow had died on the way. So either the cow was lost or dead and, as for now, there was no cow.

So far, the canopies were mostly set up, and there was a bunch of musicians at the entrance to the compound busy setting up. People were beginning to arrive, there was no food, the music hadn't started, they had only that morning picked up the casket from the shop and were taking it to the mortuary, and no senior members of the family were around. They were beginning to think that the day couldn't get any worse.

Eventually, their uncle and Ochuko joined them in the

compound, and they followed them to the family's canopy. They could see a company of people under the canopies reserved for them, and they assumed that the individuals would move as soon as they explained the purpose of the canopies.

Under the Family's Canopy

The weather was hot and humid. Ogaga had already begun to sweat under the green lace he wore, and the yellow wrapper, which he had on underneath, left him feeling drenched. This was a moment for silent prayers. 'Lord, we prayed before we came out here, take absolute control'; it will be well.

There was an entourage of twelve people that walked right to the end of the large compound to the finely decorated canopies. As they closed in on the space, there were a few people sitting around on some of the chairs. All young men, so the family went up to them to explain these canopies are hired for the family to sit in. The group of young men largely ignored the family, and they started bickering among themselves.

Ogaga grew annoyed at this, and in his most polite voice went on further, 'Excuse me, but this is where the family is meant to sit, it is paid for.' This time the young men responded; they seemed to have found a target.

'What are you saying? We are not going anywhere! What is paid for? We are not going anywhere till we are given our money.'

Ogaga and the family replied, 'What money?'

'Our three hundred thousand naira. Ask Kevwe, he hasn't paid us and over our dead bodies will this funeral be holding.' They started to get up and throw chairs around. 'Look at these

130

people; they think because they come from London. Nothing is happening in this place.'

At this raucous behaviour the family decided to retreat, and Uncle Amos said, 'It is OK, we can sit at any of the other canopies.'

The older members of the family drew Ruemu and Ogaga back and away from the riotous group; some of them had started to gyrate and hype each other up, 'Let them come and move me!'

Ogaga thought to himself, 'It is well, it is well.' He felt differently; he felt sick to the pit of his stomach, and he was hovering between wearing an expression of anger and one of sadness. There may have been a little bit of hope in his expression too. Perhaps if there was an emoji for faith under emotional distress that might do the trick. The entourage walked to the left of the compound and settled underneath the middle white canopy. The beads around Ogaga's neck were starting to feel heavier. It took effort for him to keep his head looking up. He imagined he looked a bit like a camel the way he was craning his neck forward.

After having a few words with his elder brother Ruemu, he decided to try one of the other older siblings. He picked up his phone, dialled a number: 'Igho *Miguo*,' who is this? Igho answered.

'It is me, Ogaga, I hope you are well, was wondering where you were. I've just got into Kokori.'

Igho responded, 'We've picked up the coffin and we are on our way to the mortuary to pick up the body. Ese and Ben have been there since morning.'

Ogaga responded, 'I've been trying to call both of them since yesterday but couldn't up to now.'

After a sigh, Igho then said, 'Well, there is a problem, they don't have enough money to pick up the body as they need to pay the mortuary bill.'

'How much is the bill? Ogaga enquired.

'One hundred thousand naira,' Igho said.

'I'll come to the mortuary to sort it out,' said Ogaga.

'In that case I'll pick you up.' Ogaga pressed the red phone sign on his mobile, and the line went dead.

Not long after, Ruemu, Ogaga and one of their uncles, Benson, piled into Igho's red Toyota and sped to the mortuary. Ogaga sat in the front passenger seat, while Ruemu and Uncle Benson sat in the back. On the journey it was one of greeting, 'Long time no see,' and shouting, 'I can't believe this nonsense; what happened to all the money we sent?'

'Well, I don't know,' Igho said, 'they kept me out of the loop.'

'It is like all they want is your money; they don't want your opinion or even have the courtesy to keep you informed,' Ruemu said. In truth, the oldest children had always treated Igho as a bit of an outsider. He was a chid that was born out of wedlock and came to live with the rest of his father's children in Mile Twelve when he was about twenty-one years of age. He had solely been under the care of his mother up until then.

Igho sped through the roads: some straight but filled with potholes; others windy and banked on either side by tall green grass and trees. It took about fifteen minutes in all. Ogaga had his heart in his hand, as he clenched the edge of the seat as to the nature of the drive from his dad's compound to the mortuary. By the time they arrived at the mortuary it was two pm.

From the very moment he had set off from London, he

couldn't shake off this feeling that kept creeping up on him: realisation of his own mortality. But on each flight on the way here, from London to Murtala Muhammed airport in Lagos, and from Lagos to Warri, he had been praying in his heart all the way through. 'Lord, I commit my soul and all that I am to you, let your will be done'. He never counted himself as one given to fear. People usually saw him as quite bold and brave, but all he felt was uncertainty. As if the angel of death had moved next door to him.

He didn't know what scheme, what powers, or people had conspired or were conspiring against him; he couldn't trust anyone in Nigeria with regards to this burial matter. It wasn't just a question of life and death; it wasn't a question of if there was some form of spiritual vendetta against him, but even when he thought about his brothers and sisters who lived in Nigeria, he was afraid if they were trying to fleece him, use him, castigate him or whatever else that might have crossed their minds.

Since their father had died, things hadn't been the same. He didn't feel the affinity he once felt with them, where he had seen them as family, and he wanted to help them prosper in the past. In the last year he couldn't trust one word they said. He felt they were using this opportunity of their father's death to emotionally blackmail him into giving them money. They hadn't appreciated his input when he and Ruemu had suggested that the budget was too high and where was all this money going to come from? And they would say that everyone would contribute what was allocated to them.

He had strongly doubted this then, but now he saw it as them secretly saying you and Ruemu are going to pay for this, and we are going to have a fresh new house built for us besides our father's house already in Lagos. The only allies he felt he had here, were his wife, his mother and his brother Ruemu who had the same mother and father as him. Ochuko only had two sons for the late Pa Otutu.

As they started to approach the gate of the mortuary, they saw Ese outside, and they saw Ben arguing with Samson, who was a nephew to the late Pa Otutu. Ben and Samson had never got along. Samson had lived with the family back in Mile Twelve, Lagos. He no longer lived with the family, and relations had soured over the years, especially over an incident in which it was alleged he and a group of people had beaten and maltreated the late Pa Otutu when he had attended a funeral in Kokori some years ago.

'I weep for the tears of the children; I weep for the barrenness of the land; I weep for the hardness of the earth; I weep for the tumult of the times'. Ben contemplated the lyrics he had started to write down the night before, as he felt overwhelmed by the whole process. Last night he couldn't imagine how the burial itself was going to hold. *'I tried, I tried, to bring the children together...'* his lyrics continued.

At the Funeral Parlour

Something should have been done. Dreary death had been knocking early on.

'With gratitude to God Almighty for a life well spent. The family of Chief Dr Pa Otutu announce the transition to Glory of their beloved grandfather, father, brother and cousin'. Read the caption on the posters that had been sparsely distributed through the village. There was one at the entrance to the main street that forked off the main road, and there were a couple on two lamp posts as you drove towards the compound. There was no mention of the address or the time of the funeral. It featured two pictures of him. In the first picture he was dressed in regal attire; he was middle-aged in this picture: it was a picture taken when he buried his own father. There was talk of how big that celebration was. He built a house for his dad and many people were invited. He also looked the part.

It was the Nigerian way to make a show of exuberance at events; there was something about showing opulence as a way of affirming your status as a notable individual in society, this went for the rich and the poor. Some people borrowed money to have lavish weddings and lavish funeral celebrations, because that is the way they thought it should be. Ogaga didn't feel that way; his mother had always taught him to live within his means. He felt dissatisfied regarding how things had been handled.

Here were two of his elder brothers, Ben and Ese, hiding at the funeral parlour with the body. Guests were waiting for the corpse back at the compound, and the body was dressed but had no shoes on. In Urhobo culture, the corpse had to be dressed in a fine attire, with shoes, and would be buried in this attire, essentially a befitting home sending. All they had in their pockets was thirty-two thousand naira, which they had gotten from one of the younger siblings, Efe, as his donation to the process.

From the view in Igho's car, there appeared to be a man arguing with Ben, and holding his shirt. Ben was shouting loudly in his face. As they got closer, it looked like it was Uncle Samson who had been having the altercation with Ben. So there were people who knew where Ben was, and they had beaten Ruemu and Ogaga to the punch.

Uncle Benson jumped out of the car and raced towards

Ben, and said, 'Are you Ben?'

To which Ben replied, 'Yes!'

'Well, we have to go, this is not the way we do things. You are meant to be with the guests in the compound awaiting the corpse and making sure everything is in order.' He grabbed Ben's trousers by the belt straps and started dragging him. Surprisingly, giving the fact that Ben had just been quarrelling with Samson, he didn't struggle. He had a look of resignation on his face and said, 'But we haven't paid the mortuary bill.'

Ogaga replied, 'We will sort it out.'

Ben was dragged to the car and wedged in between two people. The scene was reminiscent of an arrest scene from one of those Hollywood movies. He was driven off in a separate car, heralded back to the compound, with Uncle Samson sitting on his left side, and Uncle Benson sitting on his right side.

Ese, Ruemu, Igho and Ogaga headed into the funeral parlour where, after asking what was left of the balance, Ogaga counted out some wads of naira, which he handed to Ruemu to give to Ese to complete the balance of the mortuary bill. Ese volunteered to remain till the ambulance arrived and would come to the compound then. The rest of them jumped back in the red Toyota, as Igho raced back to the compound even faster to inform one Moses, who was actually a cousin of Pa Otutu, to take the ambulance to bring the body to the compound.

On arriving at the compound, they saw Kevwe talking with some young people; the elusive brother had finally arrived. He wasn't yet dressed, he had apparently just dismounted off the back of a motorcycle and was wearing brown trousers and a green short-sleeved shirt, with black leather slippers.

They went to greet him and query him regarding the happenings and to see if everything was in order. More family from Ruemu and Ogaga's maternal village had turned up in force for the funeral; some who had only just found out queried Ochuko. 'Why didn't you tell us when this was happening?'

To which Ochuko replied, 'I didn't want to stress you. As you can see, not a drop to drink, no food to eat, things haven't even started yet.'

As the older siblings went to change, Ogaga and Ruemu returned to the canopy to take their seats and await the arrival of the corpse. Ruemu went to speak to Kevwe and then came back and said, 'Let's go and deal with the situation. You know those people said the ambulance will not be entering the compound until the debt is paid.' Kevwe also confirmed that he owed the debt, then the lights and the siren of the ambulance could be heard. The show was about to begin. It was now three-thirty pm.

The Funeral Procession
There was some hope as the ambulance driven by Moses, cousin of the late Pa Otutu, nosed into the entrance of the compound. Ogaga and his siblings hoped it would make it in and hopefully nothing would happen. They hoped it had all been talk to try to get the family to pay up; after all, everybody dies some day and has to be buried. Sense would suggest that they would respect this occasion, and at least show some etiquette, with perhaps a few more threatening words as they hopefully would have sulked their way out of the compound.

This was not the case, and from nowhere a mass of young men flung themselves in front of the ambulance; about ten of them were at the front. Either they were trying to mimic pushing the ambulance back out of the compound or they were actually pushing.

The effect was that the ambulance remained on the same spot. It is safe to assume not because of a cancellation of the energies of the young men versus the motor of this blue and white ambulance with sirens on its roof. But rather because the driver had hit an impasse. The driver himself was also allegedly owed money; however, the family had met him the evening before and agreed to settle his debts, and it had then been suggested upon him that his ambulance would bring the corpse to the compound tomorrow.

Around the sides of the ambulance, crowding around it, were other young men and women banging on the ambulance. My goodness, a village scene from another Nollywood movie: this scene had drama, noise and tension. Many onlookers watched incredulously at this scene.

The squabble was over money. The mob consisted of some that claimed one of the man's sons, who was commissioned to refurbish the house, owed them money for materials used in building the house and he hadn't paid them. The sum of the money totalled three hundred thousand naira. This was not the first such claim or threat to the proceedings of the day.

Ogaga and Ruemu had been sternly warned to remain under what was now the maternal family canopy and not go anywhere near that commotion. Well, it looked as if the rest of the family didn't need telling, they sort of stayed away. Only Kevwe came up to speak to the head of the Bakasi boys; he pulled him aside and the verdict was that the money had to be produced. The fact was their father had also just died a few weeks ago and they needed the money to bury him.

So Ruemu and Ogaga went to speak with Kevwe, who had transformed to a tax collector. He said to Ogaga and Ruemu, 'How much money do you have?'

To which Ogaga replied, 'Collect from everyone else first then tell me how much is left.'

Kevwe said, 'No, we can't do don't that, give me what you have, give me everything you have.'

This infuriated Ruemu so much who started giving him a good telling off. 'Are you OK? How can you tell him to bring everything he has? That is a very stupid thing to say. You might be my elder but that isn't right.'

'Let us calculate how much we have and how much we need.

So you are talking to me like this, Ruemu,' Kevwe said.

Ruemu replied, 'This isn't a matter of seniority or respect. The issue is this is our father. When we have finished this we will talk about respect, but it cannot work like that.'

They moved off to the side of the house where the negotiations began. Several people were there, all claiming they were owed one debt or another. As they mentioned the debt and Kevwe confirmed, Ruemu, Ogaga and Kevwe counted some money and gave it to them. Even Moses came and said, 'I'm still owed two hundred and fifty thousand naira.'

Ogaga replied, 'We've had a conversation and we've guaranteed you will be paid, so what are you talking about?' He calmed down to this comment; it looked like a guarantee from London was a good guarantee. Every debt was settled except for the main debt of three hundred thousand naira owed to the Bakasi boys. The plasterer of the tomb was paid, the young man that put two doors up was also paid, even the young man that dug the grave was paid.

Ochuko, Ruemu's mum, had sent her younger sister to the head of the Bakasi boys. She pulled their leader aside, and shoved six hundred British pounds into his hand. 'This is the equivalent of three hundred thousand naira; now tell your boys to let this procession continue.' After a few minutes the commotion died down, and the ambulance proceeded into the compound and settled by a canopy which had been placed facing the front of the house.

While the Bakasi boys and Kevwe squabbled with the main debt, an aunt of Ruemu and Ogaga came and announced she had personally paid the debt owed to the Bakasi boys in full. She had paid the equivalent in pounds: a total of £600. The head of the Bakasi boys came up behind her and confirmed this. Ogaga knew the source of the money was his mum, Ochuko. This ploy had been to get the elder siblings of Ruemu to return the money to his aunt, because they would never pay the money to his mum. Well, as time would tell, they would never pay the money to his aunt either.

The deal had been sealed, and the debts had been settled. It was confounding just how Kevwe could rack up so much debt after ten thousand pounds had been spent on this project of burying their father, and this was the state of affairs. Sixteen months in the funeral house in Kokori, a house that was non-functional, debts, and what in the eyes of many was perceived as a disgrace.

Finally, the burial could proceed, the minister who was officiating the burial was present. The mob crowd had dispersed, and the ambulance begrudgingly made its way to the centre of the compound. Blocks had been set up to rest the coffin on while the ceremony proceeded. The families returned back under the canopies or into the house. Ese and Ben had been dressing during this commotion, at times contemplating it was interesting how people could expect everything to be OK when they are not taking steps to bring things into order.

The traders and self-made merchants returned to their wares. Now there was a market; water, drinks and food would be sold. Generally, there wasn't much water or food to be found in sight throughout the large compound.

When Ben came out, all the children were summoned by the elders, and the battalions of the late Pa Otutu were gathered; not for war, but for a final exit strategy. This was the show they were to put on before their father could be laid to rest, and before this chapter of their lives could close. There is a saying that 'blessings will follow the child that honourably buries his father'. Their father had many wives, and the children had mostly grown up together and had mostly been fond of each other. This burial process had brought out many underlying issues, such as the animosity and sometimes enmity that existed between rival wives.

Then again, in Urhobo culture, after children successfully laid their parents to rest, it opened a new chapter that resulted in the elders presiding over passing over the property of the deceased to the children. Usually, the main house would go to the eldest son, and the rest of the property would be shared among the other children. No comments or plans had been made about property sharing.

One such issue which Ogaga hoped would have died with his father was of castigating a group of children against an individual or another group. It appeared that this was what Ben had taken up. 'Things were the way they are today because there was no cooperation from this woman's children, or the problem is their mother!' Such accusations were secretly thrown around, and one thing he was also starting to realise was words even spoken in secret and things done when no one was watching eventually became public knowledge to the whole family. Alliances were complicated, and when as a child it had never mattered whose mother was who, it appeared to matter now. Ben's mother's children were all clad in fine white lace and wrappers, with matching Urhobo hats and sticks. The junior wife's children also wore white but hadn't involved themselves in the sewing of the lovely lace; their attire was more fashionable and modern, with the girls wearing gowns— one even wore trousers. Whereas Ochuko's children didn't even bother with what the family colour was, they simply wore what they had. Ruemu was clad in a deep navy-blue lace and a turquoise embroidered wrapper.

The daughter that had been estranged from the family dressed in purple, right in the midst of the rest of the children. Igho also wore a lovely white lace top with silver wrapper and a traditional hat. One of the first grandsons was there in plain clothes, that is to say jeans and a short-sleeved cream shirt. He looked like he had just left his friends on the street corner and then just walked into the funeral procession.

About twenty individual offspring of Otutu were gathered in the front of the house to put on this Urhobo show. In reality it was only a small aspect of the Urhobo burial ceremony; with this family today, you were not going to get the whole shebang.

The Ceremony
'At every celebration, the old people have come to see the young people dance'.

The main ceremony began, and the children were instructed by Uncle Amos.

Pa Otutu had requested a Christian funeral. Up stepped Pastor Steven to the microphone. He introduced himself as the pastor to 'Restoration and deliverance ministry', Lagos. He began his sermon, and within five minutes Ogaga's mind had drifted off. The sermon continued for another thirty minutes. All that Ogaga remembered from it was that he acknowledged somebody had died; everyone was busy talking to each other, milling around, or biting their nails as they waited for the next process.

The musicians were in full flow. The first part of the ceremony was for all the children present and anyone else who desired to match around the coffin. The coffin was white, and the family colours were supposed to be white. It was becoming obvious to Ogaga that the colour of Urhobo burial proceedings was white. It was all to do with the saying that when a man has lived well, his burial is not a time of crying but a celebration of his life. Not that crying wasn't allowed, on the contrary Nigerians in whole make a public show of crying, and he suspected that some people over-dramatise the picture presented or even go as far as hiring professional mourners for their funeral celebrations.

Starting with Ben, they all marched round the white coffin. As they got to Pa Otutu's feet first, their steps would slow and their faces grew long as they proceeded to his body, then to what was left of his face. Many broke into tears; most of them silently, a few more loudly. Ogaga wondered what thoughts were crossing the minds of his brothers and sisters as they paraded on this procession.

His heart skipped a bit as his turn came to follow the

procession. As he came before what was left of his father's face, his heart gave out in sorrow and anger as he thought, 'What have we done? Sixteen months it took us to get here.' It was an anger that was directed at himself, loosely at the immediate family and even more at his dad's kinsmen who he thought had put stumbling blocks in the family's way. This only lasted a minute though.

Late Pa Otutu's frame filled the whole coffin. Not that the coffin was small, but that in life he had been a man of good stature, his broad shoulders still evident. The coffin was well decorated with a gold colour lining on the handing and running along the middle of the coffin. The interior of the door was embroidered with white cotton along its borders and inlaid with a velvet blue. The floor of the coffin was covered with white cotton which was arranged in the pattern of a curtain. His corpse was dressed in brown shoes and a rich white lace with silver embroidery wrapped around his now gaunt waist, which reached over his shoes.

His torso was also clothed in white; the outline of his ribs were visible denoting some decomposition had taken place. His arms were by his sides, with both palms facing forward: in the anatomical position. His chin pointed upwards, shaven, and it was evident that he was frozen in rigor mortis. The stiffness of his corpse was not easy to ignore.

His face looked like a hollow clay vessel; this had been what had startled Ogaga, not that it didn't look like him. It made the corpse appear like an earthen vessel which was starting to fall apart; there was cotton wool stuffed into the hollow of his mouth and nostrils. His eyes were hollow, and there was difficulty distinguishing the colour of his eyes, with a blackness in the hollow of where his eyes had been that was strongly different from the colour of his eyes. It felt like this was the colour of the grave.

In seeing the face, it resembled a body that had been exhumed; however, most things were still intact. On reflection, it reminded Ogaga of museum carvings he had seen in museums showing a certain ancient people from a certain ancient city. Only before him was his father, and in this moment, he felt connected to the earth in which he stood; he felt connected to his paternal grandfather who he never remembered meeting. He felt strongly that the face of his father was also the face of his grandfather. The face was also as darkened as the face of clay which had passed through the furnace.

He passed on in a certain peril of thought which fortunately lasted a few minutes. He had long developed the art of compartmentalising situations and dealing with them swiftly and mercilessly. This made him strong; he had cried a few times in his life but had never been broken; he felt emotions but was rarely ever consumed by them; the only emotion he ever gave himself fully to was love. He stood briefly on the green grass and walked on, following the rest of his siblings towards the house. The musicians were still going at it, and now the pastor stood up to give a sermon and perform the burial rites.

The children retired to the house, while the pastor took his place in front of the musicians and started his oration. He spoke about death and why everyone needs to pay attention and get themselves ready for death. Beyond that he waffled on till he started the burial rites. He must have waffled on for a good hour before announcing, 'We will now be laying to rest the body of our dearly departed father, brother, uncle, grandfather and friend, Pa Otutu.'

The children moved from within the house and its veranda to congregate at the mouth of the annex. The graveyard boys went and lifted up the coffin and brought it to the annex. And as the reading of the rites continued, they suspended the coffin over the hole in the tomb, put ropes under the coffin, and the body was gently let down into the tomb that had been dug and plastered round about. There was no headstone. No framed picture as was common in Urhobo tradition. A framed picture would be left in the sepulchre of the deceased, so that others would always be reminded of him. Ogaga thought of his maternal grandfather's tomb, which had his name inscribed at the top of the entrance. It was nicely painted and there was a beautiful photograph of him at the head of his tomb.

Here, there would be no photograph; there was no inscription, perhaps something one of the children could take upon themselves to do at a future date. Who would brave the trip to Kokori again and face the elder kinsmen? At the mouth of the tomb they all stood aside from the graveyard boys who were in this cement tomb; the only colour was the grey of the cement plastering on the walls right throughout the tomb. From the top of the black gate, the pastor concluded the rites and announced it was time for the children to pay their last respects. It was now around five-thirty pm.

He felt relief as the body had been laid down. While the body was being let down, the elder sister was crying loudly and uncontrollably. Most people didn't think this was out of grief, but most likely histrionics which were put on for the show. Uncle Amos said to her, 'Please shut up; it isn't the time for crying!'

This moment, although it brought a certain amount of pain

and sorrow, for most of the children wasn't an all-consuming sorrow. It had been sixteen months since the death and, for many reasons, some of the children didn't act like they cared much for their father when he was alive. It seemed as if a weight was slowly lifting from the shoulders of the children from the time the pastor started the burial rites. Pa Otutu had insisted on a Christian burial before he passed on,

Minister Steven started a prayer to conclude the proceedings, and at that moment one of the unsolicited vendors was shoving a photograph into the hand of Ogaga and demanding money for the picture he had taken that Ogaga hadn't asked for. After restraining himself from decorating the boy's face with punches, rather he chose some very stern words for him.

Ogaga recovered his composure in time to say amen. Pastor Steven did pray for a long time, and thank goodness Pa Otutu was already dead; he wasn't going anywhere, and everybody else was here for him.

The body was laid down, and the children filed in, picked up a shovel and scooped up sand and poured it into the grave. As each one came up and repeated this routine, they each uttered a prayer and gave thanks that it would be well with the children. They prayed that they wouldn't make the mistakes he made, they prayed that they would be greater than their father, and they prayed that the things that troubled him would not trouble them.

Onajevwe started weeping loudly at the grave site. Uncle Amos told her to shut up. She knew people were looking at her, but whatever they said, her father was gone. However, the thing on her mind was that her calabash had broken. Pastor Steven's church hadn't amounted to anything; it seemed he was only good at prayer and able to drive the congregation into a frenzy when praying, but even his prayer today was lame.

She couldn't help but to feel that her 'Moses basket' was never rescued from the Nile, every witch that knew her name hadn't died by fire, and every charm she had was gone. Pastor Steven was now a lodger in her father's previous room. Ben had told her categorically he needed to be out after the funeral because the house now belonged to him. She tried to respond; however, she was sent to the ground by a slap she woke up from five minutes later.

Not that she disagreed with him, he wasn't making any money, and he talked too much. Her head was hurting her, so the tears continued to flow.

The next stage was orchestrated by their uncle: their father's cousin Amos. He brought them out. The musicians had resumed again, and the children were to dance around the entire compound, stopping at each canopy, thanking all the parties and companies that had attended to pay their respects, and donating small amounts of cash to each party as they went around. They also greeted the elder men with some kolanut and strong drinks, and for the women they gave super malt and a crate of soft drinks.

Typically, Ben had remarked that they hadn't bought the Guinness or soft drinks that they were meant to present at the table of the elders, and the women's groups respectively. This remark was made so somebody could come up with some money to sort this problem out. Igho went out to get the soft drinks, and Ese had some money to get the Guinness. And Ogaga went to a carrier bag he brought and brought out two bottles of hot drink, specifically London gin, to set before the elders as custom demanded.

The children danced around the canopies. More accurately, marched; there wasn't much energy in their spirits for dancing. Under every canopy each child dropped a small denomination of naira i.e. twenty, fifty naira notes for the group under each canopy. There were about twenty canopies, and usually the canopies would then split up to form two or three groups so they would get more money. The drinks were also presented to the relevant groups.

As they approached the end of this particular dance, Ogaga remembered a saying he liked very much, 'May you have enough happiness to make you sweet, enough trials to make you strong, enough sorrow to keep you human and enough hope to make you happy'. He wasn't sure if he had everything in the correct balance. In his mind the old hadn't only come to see the children dance, they had come to see what they could take from the children of Pa Otutu; a place they had never given anything to.

They danced around the compound, dropping fifty and one hundred-naira notes; preferably as small as possible. They were a large entourage, so it added up to a significant amount of money by the time each of the children had filed past each canopy. After they had made their way around, they danced in celebration to the tune of the musicians. People came up to join then and to spray them, and pictures were taken.

Ogaga's wife got up and joined him in the dance. Her father and his entourage also got up and danced their way out of the compound. They gathered in groups and took photographs.

It was a relief; the funeral was coming to an end. Many of the children and guests quietly slipped away. The children, especially the ones from London, escaped as even then people were still trying to solicit money from them. Making all sorts of claims; it was disgraceful and very sad. In truth, the majority of these people were in a poor state, and they thought of nothing else but on how to get money from people.

As the initial occupants of the Sienna piled back into the vehicle, there was relief that it was over, and their minds leapt to what the next day would bring. The next day was the concluding rites, when the children were summoned to the house of the kinsmen. This was where two goats were to be slaughtered by them which was to be done in the presence of the elders of the village. Without this rite they wouldn't have felt the burial was complete.

Dennis drove Ochuko, Ruemu, Ogaga and his wife to their uncle's house, who lived right on the edge of Kokori. They rode back with a silent contentment.

Beneath the Palm Fronds

The next morning, Dennis drove them to Uncle Amos's house. He pulled up in front of the house. As the car was pulling in, the herd of goats that had been casually sauntering in the compound dispersed from the path of the car. The occupants came down. Ogaga, Ruemu, Ochuko and Ogaga's wife followed Uncle Amos to the side of the house where he directed them to sit down.

There were two benches that lay perpendicular to each other; between the benches was a bottle of schnapps with roots inside, and a small glass covering it. It apparently was waiting for Uncle Amos. Uncle Amos was a legend. Rumour has it that he had a glass as an eye opener in the morning, and he continued till he had drained a bottle by the end of the day. It was a surprise that he spoke coherently most of the time and was able to keep his balance on the road.

In essence, he was always drunk to one degree or the other. Whether this affected his judgement was open for debate. This behaviour had gone on for so long that who could tell what his real nature was? To top it all off, he was a teacher at the local school—lucky students! Their classes must be a lot of fun. Perhaps if he taught science, he could be a living example on the effects of alcohol on the human body.

They sat down and were joined by wife number six, Vick, who wasn't lodged very far away. They had come to discuss the final rites of the burial.

'Do you know,' Uncle Amos began, 'that it was your father, Otutu, that donated the big bell for the church? Yes, that Catholic church up the road. He was very good friends with the catechist.'

'What about the school he built for the community?' Vick said.

'Well, I teach there still,' Uncle Amos said. 'You see, your father trained us. He, at a time, wanted me to come to Lagos with him, but my elder brother refused. He gave his parents a big send off. You children haven't seen the house he built for his father.'

'What about the farm?' Ochuko jumped in. 'The compound where they laid him to rest is nothing compared to the size of that farm. In those days the farm was thriving, from rearing chicken to growing yam, plantain and the rubber trees. He has done a lot for the community here, and beyond. I still remember the story he told of how he got himself educated. He healed the headmaster's son with his herbs, and from that day his tuition, till he finished secondary school, was free.

'To also think of how he got his first big job in Central Bank of Nigeria. He also cured the manging director's wife with his herbs, and that is how he got his job. He did very well; the only child of his mother, rising through society. The significant thing was that he made a huge difference in many people's lives.'

This particular topic pattered out, and they talked about the closing process of the whole ceremony. Uncle Amos mentioned what needed to be done to satisfy the customs of the elders. They needed to buy some hot drinks, soft drinks and two young goats. These, the elders will kill and cook with. After money had been deposited in his hands, Uncle Amos got up and went to buy the necessary requirements. The crowd dispersed and got ready to make their way to meet the elders.

Two hours later, the whole family gathered at Pa Otutu's cousin's house. This was where the goats would be slaughtered and where the final ceremony of the send-off would take place. As they all sat down, various groups congregated around the family. They came complaining that they never had their share of gifts at the funeral. The young men came saying they were not even given food to eat, not even a bottle of water; the family must drop something.

Uncle Amos got up and started to promise each group that everything would be sorted, that they shouldn't worry. He had already started to drink from the bottle of whisky which was for the ceremony. He repeatedly shifted from one foot to the other, attempting to steady himself as he lost his balance over and over again whilst standing.

A certain man in the crowd stood up and told him to shut up and sit down. Uncle Amos became very angry, wagging his long right index finger at him. He started hurling insults at this man, Samson, who was also a kinsman of the family. The man hurled insults back, stepped into the circle and faced him. They hurled insults at each other, spitting in each other's face as they spoke; they both seemed to have poor control of their cheeks and facial muscles.

Uncle Amos pushed the guy. Samson pushed him and slapped him on the back. Uncle Amos went into histrionics; his left hand immediately reached onto his scapula and he screamed '*Wo wegba tiyun obukome* (he has slapped me with power on the back).' The family watched in horror at the show before them, nothing that was supposed to happen was happening.

There were new tax collectors, and the master of the ceremony was causing chaos. Ochuko and Vick got up and went to speak with a cousin older than Amos. Joseph came and ushered Amos out of the circle. He came back in, and after organising a collection for the young men and women, he poured hot drink for the whole family to drink, then they slaughtered the goats.

The burial rites were now concluded. To the right of the gathering, Amos and Samson were now dancing jovially with one another. Now the children found it funny, but it wasn't funny before. Now they would have no reason to have to answer to the elders.

As the elders departed, Ogaga noted there was no mention of sharing of his father's properties. He owned a large farm in Kokori besides the compound where his house was. He also owned other houses in Delta state, besides his house in Lagos. He wasn't bothered, completing the process was more than enough for him.

The Children's Meeting

The process was now complete; the elders had killed their goats. The youth of the town had haggled for their share of the burial spoils. 'If there was ever a thing, don't worry about it,'

Ochuko said to her sons. 'They are wretched and poor; funerals and marriages represent their opportunity to squeeze people for money.'

Ruemu replied, 'The surprising thing about it is that none of them will be any better off for it. It clearly was a case where people oppress others to their own detriment. It is an ethical dilemma. It is one thing oppressing others when you are in power: you have money and influence. It is another, oppressing someone when you are poor and you happened to be in a position of temporary power due to circumstances, and herd pressure.'

As the ceremonies had all drawn to a close, the children were ready to make their exit and get their minds ready to leave the village. They stood up and embraced each other. They busied themselves taking selfies and group pictures. They didn't know if they would meet like this for a long time. As strange as it seemed, many of them had not seen their father for many years, and with him gone, it looked as though the glue that held them together was gone. Perhaps the glue had been silently melted away, and not until he passed did they realise he was the sole reason they were all brothers and sisters; now they looked a bit more like step-brothers and sisters. Each faction maintaining their mother's gate and fighting for the interest of their faction.

They began to share stories and memories they had with Pa Otutu.

Irhorho, the youngest daughter of the first wife said, 'There are countless memorable moments you know. There was one very funny, quite peculiar, event! I think when I was about seven years of age, at this time if you guys remember, Ify just moved in to the compound (Ify was the daughter of a tenant). Dad detested seeing us downstairs, and even more in a tenant's house. We also were not to collect anything from strangers. On this fateful day, knowing all these things Dad frowns at, Ify, who was about my age group as you know, talked me into collecting a strange fruit from her. Later on, that week, we had a little disagreement, and she said she would tell my dad I had been to her apartment and I ate her fruit. Suddenly, I burst out in tears as she made a further attempt to go. I began crying out and, unknowingly for me, Dad was in the sitting room downstairs. He heard my voice and called for me. I hurried to him, still crying seriously. When I got to him, I confessed what I did and how Ify threatened to report me at this point. I expected Dad to throw something at me, but instead he calmly asked me to come to him and he carried me on his thighs and he leaned my head towards his chest and wiped my tears. He asked me to stop crying and that I should not do that again. I ended up playing with his chest nipple, and he carried me for a long time. That memory of him has stuck in my mind all these years.'

Everyone burst out laughing and chorused, 'For real?'

'Yes, it is true,' she replied as more laughter and back slapping followed. It was mostly the younger children around now; the eldest children had scurried off back to their hotel in Warri. The younger children only realised this when they went to look for them to talk about all the events that had preceded the funeral and how they thought everything went. Ruemu said exasperatedly, 'For a family and culture that values gerontocracy, clearly our elders have made mistakes. They don error.'

Only Igho remained. He had joined in the picture, giving words of advice. 'Guys, make sure you check on one another;

make sure you look after each other; call each other if you are struggling; call me.'

Ogaga recalled a moment in his childhood. He was going to church on a Sunday morning. As he started walking past the side of the house, he came past the veranda, and Pa Otutu was sitting there. After Ogaga had greeted him, he asked, 'Where are you going?'

'I'm going to church,' replied Ogaga.

'You look a little bit lean. I don't think you should go today, go and rest.' Ogaga turned around and returned into the house. The truth was he was running late for church already and it would be a twenty-minute walk before he got to the outskirts of the town where the church was located, so he was glad to go back.

As people say, don't count the years, count the memories; it was obvious that for all the years, all the children, the gaining of wealth and losing of it, there were not enough memories among those that were left behind, perhaps maybe not for his children. Or maybe perhaps they just had to keep sharing. For many years Ogaga often recalled this one moment, and it was always to him a moment of endearment between him and his father. Though he had numerous conversations with his father, the only other moment he connected with his father during conversation in a deeply affectionate way was when he sat with him on the edge of his hospital bed seventeen months ago. It felt like a heart to heart; truly a great man had come home.

Oke'awo wie' we, wo vwie, ikuo jobi kwe. Yverhe akpo tai woda gbu ikwo jobi vwie, wo kwe.' *When you were born, you were crying and everyone around you was smiling. Live your life so at the end, you're the one who is smiling and everyone around you is crying.*

Epilogue

The journey onwards

The driver drove away from Warri, and they were now approaching Benin. Mr Yakubu was sitting in the passenger seat. The car radio was playing the sounds of 'Mr Eazi', 'baby they confuse me with her bum bum…'. This made Mr Yakubu chuckle; last night he had been in bed with Modupe; now she was in the back seat looking very sheepish.

'Driver! Remember we are stopping by my friend's place to pick up something.' The driver nodded to show that he had heard. After signalling to the right, he pulled off the freeway, taking the exit towards Benin.

They pulled into a compound, and Mr Yakubu said to the occupants of the car, 'Come out, let's stretch our legs while I greet my friend.' The driver and Mr Yakubu stepped out; Modupe also opened the back door. The windows at the back were tinted so that you couldn't see who was sitting at the back. The handbrake was up and the car was stationary.

Mr Yakubu put his sunglasses on, looked up and there was a very dark man who waved back at him, then he made a signal to someone who must have been behind Mr Yakubu. As Modupe turned around to see who it was, a yellow handkerchief was placed over her nose and mouth; she was surprised and her eyes widened with fear, then rage.

As she struggled to break free, she realised that the hands holding her were really strong; she tried to appeal to Mr Yakubu, still not fully cognoscente of what was happening, and all she saw was a pair of shades observing the obviously illegal activity that was taking place.

As it dawned on her that there was some noxious substance in the handkerchief causing her to start to lose her consciousness, it also dawned on her that this was Mr Yakubu's doing, as he looked at her, without even a smile or a smug look on his face, it clearly wasn't personal. The last thing she saw before losing consciousness was the black shades standing over her.

Mr Yakubu walked up to Captain, the very dark man. He brought out a thin brown envelope from his back pocket and placed it in Mr Yakubu's hand. 'As I said, this is small chops.'

'Well, I only came to get my small portion of manna which fell from heaven,' Mr Yakubu replied back. He put his sunglasses back on, turned around and went back to the vehicle.

The vehicle that entered the compound in Benin departed without the back occupant. The tinted windows were wound up. If there was anyone following them they would be none the wiser that there was ever an occupant at the back. Even at the burial, Mr Yakubu had instructed Modupe to remain in the car and not come out, in case one of the children spotted her.

On the veranda on the first floor in the compound, one of the Kawere boys held Brohen by the neck, forcing him to watch what was happening below. Brohen's knees buckled beneath him as he saw Bender smother the woman with his yellow handkerchief, pick her up and put her in the boot of the 4x4 in the middle of the compound. It seemed like it was time to go.

Captain looked up and saw Brohen's face. He was satisfied that the recruitment process was progressing well. Brohen was a smart kid: he would be brains rather than brawns and he would send him to school. Well, he could spare a bit following the payout following the ransom payout for the *oyinbo* missionaries which both the British and Nigerian governments would deny on the news.

All that would be said is 'missionaries successfully released, glad to be back in the UK with their family.'

Mr Yakubu's driver drove silently with a straight face. The sound of the radio had changed: 'chop my money, chop my money o…' by P-Square was now blaring from the radio.

Mr Yakubu had made up his mind; he thought he could legitimise his criminality as he was planning to run as a local councillor. However as situations had not panned out as planned, he would bring the syndicate back together one more time. To think that the death of his enemy would defeat him. No! This was a job for the syndicate he thought, as he pulled his mobile phone from his pocket.